Love at First Beat

Love at First Beat

A SMALL-TOWN COWBOY DOCTOR / CURVY GIRL
ROMANCE

ROUGH & READY COUNTRY
BOOK TEN

ENGRID EAVES

Chapter One

DREW

Ophir City Hospital's sprawling campus is evergreen tree-lined with a helicopter pad to one side. The main entrance has a loading and drop-off zone with a covered walkway decorated with Christmas lights. I park as close as I can to the automatic glass doors, trying to avoid the piles of snow in the parking lot and the shiny black patches of ice.

Pulling my puffy purple jacket tightly around me, I pick my way carefully towards the sliding glass doors, which open onto an expansive hallway with a round desk in the center. Two receptionists sit inside it, and both have a line. I try to breeze past, not sure what the people in line are waiting for, only to have the receptionist with steel-gray hair and thick tortoiseshell glasses holler, "Excuse me, ma'am, but you need to present your ID before entering the hospital."

"Oh, I already know where I'm going," I reply with a forward motion of my hands.

She shakes her head. "It doesn't matter. We'll still need to see your ID and give you a name badge."

I sigh, hunching forward a little bit. No matter which line

I choose, I have three people in front of me. My impatience grows as I watch the women chat heartily with each person as they present their identification.

Usually, I appreciate the human touch of having live receptionists instead of an automated computer check-in. But right now, I need to get to my boyfriend's hospital bed. He called yesterday to tell me he couldn't make it for Christmas due to a skiing accident. But something feels off about his story—namely, the fact he doesn't ski. Or at least, never expressed an interest in the sport to me.

We've been in a long-distance relationship for the past year that feels like it's going nowhere. It all started when he took a job as an MRI technician, relocating from Los Angeles to Ophir City. My friends wonder why I'm still with him, and I question this myself, sometimes. I guess I fell in love with the idea of what I thought he could be. And he's charming and fun, the life of the party... Dating him feels like riding a roller-coaster—filled with heady highs and stomach-churning lows. Maybe I'm addicted to the adrenaline of it all...even though in my heart of hearts, I know he doesn't treat me right. Yet, I keep hoping he'll change. Hope is the drug of fools.

Still, Reggie sounded so sad on the phone, which makes a part of me intensely guilty for doubting him. But when I offered to visit and spend Christmas with him at the hospital, he refused, saying he didn't want to ruin my holidays. If it's selfless consideration on his part, I'll feel terrible about my suspicions. Based on his record of cheating, though, I can't shake my skepticism.

I stand in line for so long that my mind starts wandering—far from a new state for me. Visions of good-looking doctors wooing sassy nurses or adorable patients fill me head. Soon, I've got Shonda Rimes-style medical drama plots brewing. An illicit scene in a patient's room or maybe the break room. My eyes dart around the hospital entry, finding countless possibilities...

"Ma'am, who are you here for?"

I shake my head, realizing it's my turn and trying to clear the fantasy fogging my thoughts. I step forward to the kiosk. "Sorry about that. Reginald Tate. He should be in room four thirty-five."

"I'll need to see photo ID..." the gray-haired woman with tortoiseshell glasses says, her voice wandering off as she looks at her computer screen. Her brows knit, and her face scowls.

I dig through my original Gucci canvas tote with purple leather trim, find my matching purple wallet, and open it.

"No, I'm sorry, Ma'am, but there's no patient by that name at this facility."

"It's Reginald Tate," I repeat impatiently, spelling out the name. "He also works in radiology. He's an MRI tech."

She pushes her glasses up on her nose and shakes her head. "A skiing accident, you say? Hmm... Sorry, but nobody by that name checked into this hospital."

"It should be room four thirty-five."

"So you've said." She nods, pressing her mouth firmly together.

I put my driver's license on the kiosk desk, and she shakes her head.

"And you've checked all the patients in the hospital?"

"Yes, and I found no one by that name."

I shrug, taking back my ID and returning it to my wallet. "This is the only hospital in Ophir City, right?"

She nods.

"I just drove nearly seven hours from Los Angeles. I don't know what's going on, and I'm hungry and tired. Is there any place I can sit down for a moment to text him and figure everything out?"

"There's a cafe over there. I can give you a general guest badge if you like?"

"Yes, thank you." I pull my ID back out and sign in.

"Let me know if I can help you with anything else," she says with an ambivalent face that looks like she's already judging me.

I walk over to the Starbucks cafe and place my order. "A hot venti Americano with cream and some of your bacon and gruyere egg bites, please."

"Will that be all?" The perky twenty-something barista behind the counter asks, shaking her chin-length blonde bob when she talks.

"Yes, that'll do it. Thank you."

Maybe if I eat something, I won't feel so shaky or frustrated. I make my way over to an empty table with two chairs, setting down my purse and laptop bag that I carry everywhere. After all, I never know when inspiration will strike.

Opening my phone, I read through my last string of texts with Reggie.

> I'm in room 435... If you call rn I'll pick up. But they've got me on strong meds so I'll be out within the next 30 min or so

After that text, I called immediately, and he picked up on the second ring. So, I know with one hundred percent certainty he was here yesterday. Maybe he's been discharged?

I text:

> Are you still in room 435? What's going on?

I wait impatiently as three dots light up the screen, letting me know he's texting back.

A cheery female voice pulls me out of my phone, declaring, "Venti Americano with cream and bacon and gruyere egg bites."

I stand up, marveling at how quickly they got my order ready. Of course, Ophir City's small beans compared to Los Angeles, so everything's likely faster here. At the pickup counter, I reach for my bacon and gruyere egg bites, colliding with a big, burly white man's hand.

"Excuse me," I grumble indignantly.

Looking at the man beside me, I notice his gorgeous square-cut jaw and indigo eyes. He's clean-shaven with a buzzed haircut and perfect posture. Everything about him screams military. But he's wearing aqua-colored hospital scrubs, and his name badge reads Fletcher Knight, Cardiologist.

The man eyes me with an exasperated scowl. "You're excused."

Both of us reach for the egg bites again. Now, I really get annoyed, even though he's hotter than hell with a straight, proportionate nose, highly kissable full lips, and a muscular physique barely concealed beneath his scrubs.

"Those are *my* egg bites," he says, raising a challenging eyebrow.

"No, they're my egg bites, and the Venti Americano with cream is mine, too."

His eyes narrow, and he frowns deeply. "I don't know what trick you're playing, but that's my Venti Americano with cream, actually," he replies firmly, grabbing the drink and sack of food.

What are the odds that we have the exact same order back to back? I feel like I'm on one of those practical joke reality shows.

Suddenly, the barista appears with a second Venti drink and a sack of egg bites. "Another order of bacon and gruyere egg bites with a hot Venti Americano with cream."

Our eyes meet, really looking at each other this time. An embarrassed, incredulous grin captures my mouth. But the man continues frowning, the walking personification of annoyance.

The tone of his voice matches his appearance. "I'm pretty sure I ordered first because I watched you walk over. But we can ask the barista if you're not happy with receiving the second order."

Watched me walk over? My heart flutters in my chest.

"Hey Julie, can you clarify the orders for us, please?" the man barks, furrowing his brows.

The barista nods. "Two back-to-back Venti Americanos with cream and bacon and gruyere egg bites."

"Yeah, but who ordered first? We're trying not to mix up our orders."

"You did, Dr. Knight."

The man has a stick so far up his ass that the statement makes me laugh. *Really? Ask the barista which of the exact same orders were intended for each of us?*

"You heard, Julie. I was first. Are you good now?"

I chuckle in disbelief. "I'm fine."

"Yes, you are," he grumbles before turning around to walk away. Although his words sound flirtatious, the way he pronounces them and then exits feels like a slap in the face. Nevertheless, my eyes follow him shamelessly, honing in on his tight, round ass. I've never seen someone make a pair of scrubs look so good.

The barista leans over the counter. "That's our resident hottie. Good-looking, isn't he?"

"Girl, that's the understatement of the year," I reply, fanning myself. "And here I thought he was some creep, stealing my order."

She shakes her head. "Nope, you ordered the same things one after the other. "What are the odds of that?"

I shake my head, making my way to my seat. Apparently, the odds are much better than finding the boyfriend who's been swallowed whole by Ophir City Hospital.

Taking a seat, I neatly spread out my egg bites to cool and take a tentative sip of coffee, pleasantly surprised by the ideal sipping temperature that greets my tongue. Rifling through my bag again to find my phone, I see a new message from Reggie.

> Yep, still in the hospital. There's no way I'm going to make it down your way. But I've got my cell charged again. So, use that when calling. That way, I'll be sure to pick up. I don't always hear the hospital phone ring

> 435, right?

> Yeah, but like I said, my cell's the best way to reach me now that I have it charged

Something about this situation stinks to high heaven. I eat my egg bites silently, my appetite waning by the end. A sudden apprehension leaves me uncertain I want to know anymore. But I didn't drive seven hours to leave without answers. Either Reggie's lying or the hospital can't keep track of its patients.

I spend a few minutes studying the elevators across from the Starbucks, realizing that I could easily slip into one without the name badge ladies noticing. It's the only way to know with certainty what's really going on with Reggie.

Chapter Two

FLETCHER

"**H**ey, doc!" Molly says cheerfully as I roll by with my coffee and food bag in hand.

"I'm finishing my break, and then I'll begin making rounds."

Molly has a mane of black curls barely restrained by her ponytail, and her cheeks always turn bright red when we talk. I don't mean to sound conceited but that happens with a lot of women in the hospital. It's a strange experience after fourteen years in the military, with seven years at Army hospitals. Flirting there was nonexistent.

"You won't believe what happened at the Starbucks downstairs," I say, stopping to talk to her. I don't know why I'm telling her this story. Maybe because the order stealer downstairs is the first woman who's taken my breath away in years. All I know is from her curly, raven-hued chin-length bob to her generous lips and even more generous curves, I can't remember the last time a woman's appearance got my full attention like that...

If it's ever happened at all...

Of course, this is the last thing my on-again, off-again girl-

8

friend of five years, Mandy, would want to hear. But we've been broken up for a month now, and I mean to keep it that way. At least, that's the plan.

"I went for my normal drink and food order, and this woman tried to steal it from me."

"Seriously?" Molly asks, her face screwing up with concern.

"Yeah, and when I questioned what was going on, it turned out she ordered the exact same thing as me."

Molly looks less than impressed, so I add, "You don't get it. I always order a hot Venti Americano with cream and bacon and gruyere egg bites. What are the odds that someone would order the exact same thing right after me?"

"Weird." She frowns. "Hold that thought. I have someone trying to come in."

Molly pushes the intercom button. "How may I help you?"

"I'm trying to visit a patient in room four thirty-five."

I immediately recognize the voice, although I only heard it for the first time less than twenty minutes ago. Looking at the video feed, I welcome the sight of the curvy, ebony-skinned beauty. "That's the woman who tried to steal my order. I mean, who ordered the same thing as me. Let her in."

Molly's eyes flash towards mine quizzically before she pushes the entrance button.

"I'm headed to the break room, but then I'll be around." I nod curtly, striding down the hallway before the lovely woman and I cross paths again.

The break room is nothing to write home about. And fans of shows like *Grey's Anatomy* would be highly disappointed. It has a lounge area with the most uncomfortable furniture I've ever sat in, although it has a tranquil vibe. Decorated in shades of pale blue, green, and pink, it exudes a calming, almost sedated vibe. Personal lockers line one wall where we put our belongings while on shift. Next to the lockers are a couple of vending machines that pump out the unhealthiest food on the planet, but at least there's a Keurig with an endless supply of K-cups, so I can always get my caffeine fix.

A flat-screen TV on the wall stays perpetually tuned to CNN, although I hardly ever see anybody willfully hanging out in this room. Most hospital staff prefer the cafeteria, which makes this place my go-to spot when I want privacy and peace. As a full-time cardiologist with the hospital, I easily work sixty hours a week, which makes the search for solitude a constant.

The break room includes several small, separate, quiet rooms where nurses and physicians can take quick naps as needed. Sparsely furnished, each room contains a bed and a desk. I take advantage of these rooms more than anyone. After fourteen years in the military, I can sleep anywhere. As for my favorite part of the hospital, it would have to be the gym, located on the first floor. I utilize the facility before or after work most days. After all, nothing drives home the need to remain physically fit better than working with patients whose lifestyles have landed them in the hospital. And a regular fitness habit goes with the whole military MO, too.

My phone vibrates against my leg, and I retrieve it, shaking my head and frowning deeply. I stare at a text from Mandy, hesitating about whether I even want to open it.

I have no trouble being in combat zones, operating on patients in the most primitive conditions, and risking my life. But communicating with my on-again, off-again girlfriend is another matter entirely. One that makes my pulse pound and my stomach knot. Neither in a good way.

I know we're broken up and all. But why
can't I use the ski lodge one more time? It's
not like you ever have the time to go up
there anyway. Besides, it's the least you
can do after five years wasted on a dead-
end relationship

Five years wasted? Even though I consider myself a tough
bastard with a thick exterior, her words sting.

Last time I checked, you're the one who
threw the past five years away with your
poorly timed breakup

You should've kept me around until after
the holidays if you wanted to use the ski
lodge so badly

Mandy's an MRI tech who works in the radiology department on the first floor. She covers the swing shift during the
weekdays, so I wonder if she has tomorrow, Wednesday, off
since it's Christmas.

You sound mad, Fletcher

Not mad.

Done.

I've heard that before

Yeah, well, this time it's different

It has to be different, I remind myself, because Mandy
crossed a line. She cheated on me. Although it wasn't physical,
she admitted to having an emotional affair with one of her
coworkers.

11

> What? You can't find a better love shack for you and Reggie?

My stomach knots.

> You know jealousy is unattractive

Her last response infuriates me more than she should still be able to do. We broke up during Thanksgiving when she got drunk enough at her family's house to confess everything to everyone. And by everything to everyone, I mean even her preschool nieces and nephews know she cheated on me because I'm "emotionally unavailable." Fun times.

It was hardly the way I wanted to spend one of my rare days off. But in all five years of dating, she never spent much time worrying about what I wanted, so I don't know why this surprises me. As my foster brothers keep pointing out, the only person capable of stopping this vicious cycle is me. In truth, I checked out of the toxic relationship a long time ago.

But work keeps me so busy I don't really have time to move on. So, when I get lonely, it's easier to go back and repeat the same mistakes rather than try something new. That whole devil you know thing, I guess... I'm also exhausted by the idea of getting acquainted with a brand-new person. One whom I'll have to try to figure out, habituate myself to, and learn to trust. None of these areas are among my strong suits.

> We're done, so it goes without saying I no longer care about what you do and don't find attractive

> Falling back into your petty old ways.
> Whatever, Fletch

My finger hovers over my phone screen as I try to think up

the cleverest, meanest way to reply. After a few moments of indulging this childish impulse, I let her last comment go. Because I really am done this time.

As a physician, I would love to turn off my phone and not be beholden to it. But I have to stay on top of my calls. So, instead, I block Mandy's number. Although I expect the move to be bittersweet, it feels strangely liberating. Although far from the first time I've done this, for some reason, it feels like it will stick this time.

Throwing away the bag that my egg bites came in, I set my coffee cup on top of the refrigerator to finish later. Then, I head back to work, wondering if I'll get another glimpse of the gorgeous woman who came to visit Anton Horowitz in room four thirty-five. I don't know what the lucky old bastard did to get a visit from her. But I'd be lying if I said I didn't want another chance to check her out and speak with her.

Chapter Three

I enter four thirty-five, pausing near the door for my eyes to adjust to the room's dimness. A curtain conceals most of the window along the back wall, shutting out its light. But I can see the top left-hand corner of the window frame, where white snow swirls in chaotic circles. All day, meteorologists on my satellite radio warned of the atmospheric river about to descend upon us. Each passing moment proves their forecasts more likely.

After taking a few deep breaths, I put on my biggest smile, trying to shake the ominous feeling inside. Rounding the curtain, I prepare to see a bedridden Reggie, his leg in a cast and misery written on his face. I hope my unexpected presence will put a smile on his face. But no matter what, I'm here for him, even if he prefers complaining and staying in a bad mood.

"Hi, baby, I couldn't—" I freeze, staring at the occupant of the room's one bed. He's an old, wizened white man with thinning gray hair and an oxygen tube in his nose. He wears a white and blue hospital gown that makes him look incredibly frail, and his paper-thin skin hangs loosely on his arms. An IV sticks out of one arm, and a blood pressure cuff remains on the other.

His big, black eyes scrutinize me as I stammer, "I'm sorry. I must have the wrong room."

"What room are you looking for?"

"Four thirty-five."

"This is the right room. Have a seat, young lady." The man speaks slowly and confidently with a practiced air that immediately feels like I'm in the presence of greatness. His persuasiveness and inherent authority make me press my lips tightly together and sit down despite myself.

"It's been a long time since I had a woman call me 'baby,' and I'm not sure what Gracie would think about it. God rest her soul. Actually, that's a lie," he says, chuckling. "I know exactly what she'd say. She'd tell you to keep your hands off her man. But she's been dead so long sometimes I have to stare at her photos to remember what she looks like. It's a damn shame when time steals the image of your wife from you."

I exhale, pressing my hands together in my lap. I open my mouth to reply when the elderly man starts chatting again.

"That said, I must confess, hearing 'baby' has put a new warmth back in my heart. A warmth I thought I'd never feel again. Thank you, Miss." He presses the adjuster on his hospital bed, which raises the back enough for him to lean forward and offer his hand. "I'm Anton Horowitz. Former concert pianist and current heart failure patient."

I take his shaky, cold hand, covering it warmly with both of mine. "And I'm Drew O'Day. You feel cold, Mr. Horowitz. Can I have the nurses bring you some more blankets? You know, if you request it, I'm pretty sure they'll heat them in the dryer for you."

"That sounds like a decadent idea, my dear. I like it."

Standing up, I poke my head into the hallway until I catch a passing nurse's attention, explaining my request. A few minutes later, the nurse returns with a handful of warm linens, tucking the old man in until he looks like the Cheshire Cat—all smiles.

"Now, this is the life," he sighs. "So, what have I managed to do right in this world to have a gorgeous dame like you walk into my hospital room?"

I let go of his hand, and he looks slightly disappointed as I sit back in my chair. "Well, I'm here to see my boyfriend, Reggie. He called me yesterday from this very hospital, in this very room, claiming to be here with a skiing injury. He said he couldn't spend Christmas with me because of it."

"Oh, Reggie," the old man says with a laugh. "Very nice, good-looking black guy with a beard. He works in the X-ray department or something along those lines. I told him I'd like my beard like his, and he gave me the card of a barber proficient at the look...I'm trying to remember what he told me to ask for..."

"A fade?"

"Yes! That's it," the man says, clapping his hands together. "Now, give me your honest opinion, young lady. Am I too old to pull off said fade, or do you think it would look good on me?"

I cock my head to the side, making a show of examining his face. Finally, I say, "I think it would look good. You know, really bring out your rugged jaw and the angular lines of your face."

"More like the sucked-up skinny old guy parts of my face."

"No," I shake my head, feeling momentarily lighter as I focus on him instead of my present circumstances. "It would make you look dapper."

"Just like Reggie. Speaking of your gentleman caller, we had a long talk. But I'm sorry to hear he's your boyfriend."

I frown, feeling my pulse hasten.

"Don't get me wrong. He's a likable fellow but not

marriage material. He's got a girl on the side. Told me all about her. And that's why he called from my room and made the excuses he did because he promised to spend Christmas with her this year. Apparently, he plans on sweeping her off her feet."

Tears sting the backs of my eyes, and by the end of his explanation, my hands fist in my lap. "He has a girl on the side? How do you know this?"

He shrugs. "Because I told him that if he was going to barge into my room and use my phone, the least he could do was keep me company for a while. So, yeah, we discussed women, his current situation, and what he's going to do about it. Unfortunately, he didn't take one word of my advice, and he also didn't tell me the whole truth because if I knew how gorgeous you were, I'd have told him to figure it out and find a way back to your place for Christmas. No offense, but you're a treasure. It shouldn't take old man eyes to see this."

"You know how to make a girl feel amazing," I reply, trying hard to turn the corners of my mouth up. "But I know where my shortcomings lie. Reggie always said I carried too much weight. I've been on every diet in the book...in fact, I'm doing the whole keto thing right now. And I do cardio until I beg to die. But nothing makes the pounds budge."

"Honey, I wouldn't change one thing about you. You're what guys back in the day called voluptuous or hourglass. You've got lots of curves in all the right spots. My apologies for telling you this because the last thing I want you to think is that I'm being lascivious. That said, even an old guy like me with a faint heartbeat can still recognize beauty when I see it."

I look down, my cheeks burning.

"Let's face it. Reggie's what you'd call a putz."

"A putz? Is that a technical term?" I tease, trying to hold back tears, as he nods firmly.

The old man leans forward, and I almost hear him

17

groaning as he fights to cross the distance between us, patting my hand. "I'm sorry to have broken the news to you like this. But you need to know."

After a few moments, I look up, staring long and hard at the little old man. "Thank you for telling me."

"It's tough news to relay on Christmas. But there's no use in you hoping things are different. That would keep you from moving on, and believe me, you *need* to move on. Reggie's fun to talk to but you deserve better. Much better."

I nod, twisting my hands in my lap. "I'm still trying to understand exactly what you're telling me here. So, Reggie let himself into your room yesterday to talk to me on the phone."

"That's right," he replies, shaking his head, "It was the darnedest thing. But clever. I'll give him that."

"I should have known better. You know, this isn't the first time he's cheated on me or disrespected me. Fool me once, shame on you; fool me twice, shame on me."

"Yeah, but you can't let the other woman off the hook, either. I don't know much about her, but she works here at the hospital with Reggie."

"Really?" Now my blood's boiling.

"Yeah, they're going on a ski vacation, so he wasn't lying about that part. But he isn't injured, and you know the rest. So, I'll save my breath."

"You know what the worst of it is?" I ask, waiting until Mr. Horowitz nods. "I drove more than six and a half hours from Los Angeles to surprise him and spend Christmas with him in the hospital. How could I be such a fool?" Emotion finally grips me, and I bite my generous lower lip hard, fighting sobs.

"You took him at his word because you're a good person. A loving and generous person, I'd wager. You're not the problem. He is."

I shrug, wiping at my cheeks.

"You know, there's a saying for this. Don't cast pearls before swine."

"I guess that makes me the pearls and Reggie the swine?"

"Bingo."

A courtesy rap sounds at the door before it squeaks open, and I hear rubber soles on the squeaky linoleum. "Good evening, Mr. Horowitz," a rich voice says. One that sounds oddly familiar. "I'm turning up the lights, so close your eyes if necessary."

The room brightens, and a robust and muscular arm draws back the divider curtain, revealing my nemesis from Starbucks. He stands directly across from me on the opposite side of Mr. Horowitz's bed, frowning at me. "Well, if it isn't the egg bites thief. Fancy seeing you again."

"I didn't steal your egg bites. I ordered the same thing. There's no law against that."

"The exact same thing," he says, narrowing his gaze at me. "By the way, I didn't get to introduce myself earlier. Pardon my manners. I'm Dr. Fletcher Knight." He comes around the side of the bed to shake my hand firmly.

I stay seated, frowning as I reply, "The name's Drew O'Day."

His hand is large and rough, and my flesh shivers with unprecedented delight at his warm touch. His eyes widen, and his face betrays a hint of surprise, which makes me wonder if he feels it, too.

"You are not," he replies, shaking his head.

"I'm not what?"

"You're not Drew O'Day. Dr. Knight and Ms. O'Day? There's no way."

I nod, shrugging. "It's not my fault if you've got a weird last name."

"Knight and O'Day... What's the universe trying to tell us?"

I shrug, realizing we're still holding each other's hand. It should be an awkward recognition, but for some reason, I'd be happy if he never let go.

"Are you Irish? Or perhaps married to an Irishman?" He turns my hand over, spying the lack of a ring and pressing his lips together with an expression akin to satisfaction.

"I'm of Irish and Jamaican descent. One generation enough removed to speak without an accent. But I can still make a mean jerk chicken and Sorrel tea you won't soon forget."

"Jamaica doesn't sound half bad right about now," the handsome doctor replies, looking forlornly out the window. "Apparently, we're getting the atmospheric river meteorologists promised earlier."

"It sure does look like it," Mr. Horowitz seconds, looking out the window.

"Well, that's just great," I reply as the doctor finally lets go of my hand, and I go back to clutching both tightly in my lap.

Chapter Four

"**W**hat's just great?" I ask grumpily, eyeing the stunning woman seated in front of me and trying like mad to figure out what it is about her that seizes my heart and won't let go.

My hand itches to touch her thick, curly black locks and even more so to palm her cheek and run my thumb over her full lower lip. She smells like sandalwood and jasmine, and her mahogany eyes have a faint smattering of amber in them that transfixes me.

"This weather. I'm here visiting from Los Angeles, which means I'm a SoCal girl and totally not cut out for driving in the snow."

I cock my head to the side, raising my eyebrow. "Ma'am, you're currently at sixty-five hundred feet in the Sierra Nevada Mountains in December. The thought never crossed your mind that you might have to prepare for snowy driving conditions?"

She lets out the most adorable little puff of air, shaking her head. "I kind of headed out on this adventure impulsively. I should've planned better. But I didn't, and that's that."

"Well, alright then." I bobble my head back and forth between her and Mr. Horowitz. "No offense, but what made you drive all the way from Los Angeles for this old guy?"

The elderly man laughs, "I'd ask the same question if I were you. Although I must say, and I'm not bragging when I admit this, I had pretty dames lining up around the block to meet me at the height of my musical career."

"I don't doubt it," the woman says in a tone so silky jealousy tightens my throat. What I wouldn't give to have her say something to me in that voice. "Women love musicians."

"Apparently I went into the wrong line of work, then," I grumble. "So, is that why you're here, Ms. O'Day?"

She laughs, shaking her head. "Oh my, no. I was here to surprise my boyfriend, Reggie. He works at the hospital, although a different department. Apparently, he came in here yesterday to use Mr. Horowitz's phone. He called me and told me he was in the hospital due to a skiing injury and wouldn't be able to drive down to my house for Christmas."

My brows furrow. "Please don't tell me you're talking about Reggie from radiology."

"He's an MRI tech."

"No fucking way," I exclaim before catching myself. "Sorry Mr. Horowitz and Ms. O'Day, but I'm former Army, so you'll have to excuse the colorful language. Fuck!"

"You know Reggie?"

I shake my head looking down at my feet. "I cannot fucking believe this. Yeah, I know Reggie."

"May I ask how?" Drew challenges, raising her eyebrow.

"My ex-girlfriend, Mandy, works with him. Apparently, she's been carrying on an emotional affair with him because I'm unavailable in the feelings department."

Pain streaks across the lovely woman's face, and she bites her bottom lip, pausing for a moment. I know exactly how she feels.

Finally, she says, "I hate to break this to you, but if it involves Reggie, I can't imagine it stopped at emotions..."

"That's a strange thing to say about your boyfriend who you drove from SoCal to see. Has he cheated on you before?"

She looks down at the hands she twists in her lap. "You could say that..."

"That doesn't make any sense," I grumble.

She looks up, searching my face.

I explain, "You're a stunning woman. Why would you settle for a lowlife like that?"

"I suppose I could ask you the same question. May I ask why you were dating her? I mean, you're a handsome man, former military, and a doctor to boot. I can't imagine you don't have women lining up."

I shrug, feeling my cheeks warm. It's intolerable. *What the hell is this woman doing to me? Am I back in middle school or something?* "When you work sixty plus hours a week, there's not a lot of time left for socializing. So, I guess I did the lazy thing and clung to what I already had..."

"Even though it doesn't sound like you ever really had it," she adds flatly.

"Yeah, I think you could make a convincing argument along those lines. But then hindsight's the only kind of vision that doesn't come in handy."

"You couldn't be more right about that," she says, nodding.

"No offense, you two, but I'd like to get whatever medical wisdom Dr. Knight has to impart," Mr. Horowitz interrupts, leaving me thoroughly embarrassed. Talk about a lack of professionalism. Yet, when I look at the old man's face, his expression looks more mischievous than peeved.

"Let me go outside while you two talk," Drew says, standing up, but the old man waves her offer away.

"Please, stay. Whatever doc has to tell me you can hear,

too. It's not like we don't all know what the final verdict is going to be—death. But then, it's coming for every single person in this room."

Drew's brows knit.

"Please, sit, pretty lady," he insists, staring at her until she plops back down. Then, turning to me, he says, "Alright, doc, lay it on me."

I raise my eyebrows. "So, I have your verbal Drew's okay to discuss medical information with? Even though you only just met her?"

He nods firmly. "I may not know her well, but I'm a good judge of character, and I can already tell she's a swell girl. And one who knows how to spoil me. She made the nurses bring me hot blankets. It was heavenly."

I nod, glancing at his chart. "Your ejection fraction rate remains at twenty percent, which is far lower than I'd like to see. It should be over the fifties at a bare minimum. This means your heart isn't efficiently pumping blood through your system, which can lead to other complications like swollen ankles and legs and excess fluid in your lungs. This is why you feel uncomfortable and have trouble breathing when you lie down. It's also why you experience shortness of breath."

"Is the official diagnosis still heart failure?"

"Yes. Although with proper care and management, you can live for years with the condition. I don't really care for the name 'heart failure' because it sounds so final. That said, if you're not willing to make the prescribed lifestyle changes, your outcome doesn't look good."

"You're full of cheerful news today, aren't you?"

"It's part of the job," I say, turning the corners of my mouth down. "Fortunately, there are medications we can put you on to potentially strengthen your heart. We can also give you diuretics to bring down the swelling in your system, but it's a careful balancing act as these medicines can negatively impact your kidneys."

"So, you're saying there's a chance for me if I'm willing to clean up my act?"

I nod firmly.

The old man shrugs, turning towards Drew. "I guess this is the best news I can expect."

She leans forward, patting his right hand reassuringly. "Yes, it sounds like you're in very good and capable hands with Dr. Knight."

I nod, side-eying the beauty for one moment before turning back to my patient. "So much about your treatment will involve lifestyle changes. But there's definitely room for improvement, which is not a prognosis that I can always deliver to my patients."

"Alright, then. I guess it could be worse. Even though, if I'm being honest, I'm ready to see my Gracie again."

I frown and so does Drew. I glance in her direction, catching her eye, and her cheeks redden. She's so fucking beautiful it takes my breath away. How Reggie could be such an idiot, I'll never know.

My only solace comes from knowing that he and Mandy truly deserve each other. I catch myself at the end of this last thought. Even a month ago, I would have never admitted such a thing to myself, but it's true, and it's damn well liberating to think about. For better or worse, meeting Drew has made me open my eyes to the world of possibilities that exist beyond Mandy. It feels like a significant step towards personal healing and growth.

"Doc, I need you to do me a favor," Mr. Horowitz says, drawing me back from my silent admiration of Drew.

"And what's that?"

The old man looks at Drew next. "I need a favor from you, too."

Great. Apprehension fills me.

She arches her eyebrows, and he raises bushy gray ones in return until she finally nods.

"You two have been through a lot at the hands of your exes, and it's no little matter that fate brought you together like this. The least you can do is agree to talk again. Maybe head to the cafe or cafeteria for a drink or some food and some clarifying conversation? It might seem like an awkward request, but trust an old man. You both need to decompress together."

To my utter surprise, I look at Drew point blank and agree with him. "He's right. I don't know how long you're staying. But maybe we could do dinner or more egg bites in a bit?"

Her face flushes, and she looks over her shoulder out the window, pressing her lips tightly together. "I'm not going anywhere in this weather. So, yes, I'll be here when you're ready, Dr. Knight."

"It's a date, then, Ms. O'Day." That's not what I meant to say. "I mean, a date like on the calendar. Not like a date...date."

"Sorry for butting in again, but considering what you've both just been through, it should be a date. Call it a revenge date, if it makes you feel better." Mr. Horowitz grins from ear to ear.

I run my hand through my hair, eyeing Drew's warm expression with satisfaction. "You may be onto something, Mr. Horowitz. Alright, I've got other patients to see. But I'll be back around in about an hour for you, Ms. O'Day, if that works?"

"Yes," she replies confidently, and I stroll out of four thirty-five feeling more excited than I have in years. It's totally irrational and makes no sense, but then nothing about my curvy new acquaintance fits neatly into the box of reason. Maybe I could use a little more mystery and allure in my life.

Chapter Five

DREW

"You've got matchmaker written all over you, Mr. Horowitz. I never would've guessed." I observe, watching the handsome doctor exit the room.

"Well, when you've lived as long as I have, you start to see patterns that you sometimes want to correct."

"Patterns? What do you mean?"

"Take you and Fletcher...I mean, Dr. Knight. You're both obviously the givers in your relationships. Always going above and beyond and doing far more for your partners than they deserve. As you driving from SoCal proves or Fletcher putting up with awful treatment from that Mandy girl."

"You've been here a while to learn so much about the good doctor's personal life."

The old man nods emphatically. "I have. But in truth, you don't have to be here long to get a load of how she treats him. He picked up his cell phone in my room once, and I could hear her berating him over the line...in the middle of his shift. It was very unprofessional behavior on her part. And then that whole thing about cheating on him because he's emotionally unavailable. Who made him that way, I wonder?"

27

I nod. "Core wounds can run deep in an individual. His may have started with her, or they may go back much further to his childhood. You know, there's got to be some reason he attracted her in the first place and has put up with her behavior for however long they've been together."

Mr. Horowitz eyes me curiously. "Are you a psychiatrist or something?"

I shake my head, chuckling. "No, I'm a romance writer."

"A romance writer? How lovely. Is it the kind of stuff an old man like me can read?"

I grimace at the thought. "While I'm sure my books wouldn't introduce you to anything you don't already know about, they are not for the faint of heart."

"And I just so happen to be among the faint of heart at this point." He chuckles.

"I so didn't mean it like that," I say, feeling abysmally awkward.

"It's fine. I get it. Your books are a little spicy for an old guy like me."

I nod. "That's a good way to put it."

"Getting back to the point I was trying to make before. It seems like givers always end up with takers. You know, emotional vampires or whatever they're calling them these days. People that will suck the life out of them. So, wouldn't it be nice for a change to see two givers get together?"

"You mean, like me and Dr. Knight?"

"Now, you're onto something," he says, clapping his hands together.

I shake my head. "Yes, but at the same time, there has to be a reason two givers don't typically get together. Maybe we don't find each other attractive. Who knows?"

"If you decided to write a new romance with that as the premise, how would it go?"

Now, he's piqued my interest. The gears in my brain turn

as I think about the plot line. "Well, there would have to be external forces against them because internal factors wouldn't be the issue so much. So, things like living in different cities, not wanting to change their lifestyles, being set in their ways and too rigid for something new..."

"Could those things be overcome in the name of love? Especially by two inherently loving, giving people?" asks the matchmaker with a mischievous grin.

I shrug. "I don't know. I mean, the long-distance thing is no small issue."

"But it wasn't a problem when the long distance involved visiting Reggie... I mean, the taker in this experiment."

I cock my head to the side, pursing my lips. "You may have a point. But I'd say it's more like this. Because of the awful long-distance relationship with the taker, the giver will never go for that dynamic again...even with a giving man. Does that make sense?"

He shakes his head, chuckling under his breath. "No offense, but your generation likes to make everything impossible, all in the name of protecting yourselves from hurts that have never happened. But wouldn't the risk of a broken heart be worth a chance at true love?"

I stare blankly at him.

"Do you want to know how I met my wife?"

"Sure."

"Gracie was the much younger wife of the conductor of the New York Philharmonic. I often played with the orchestra, and I remember her always attending rehearsals, seated in the third row back on the left-hand side, affording her excellent views of me as I played piano. Her eyes would sizzle the back of my dress coat, and when I returned her gaze, it always knocked the wind out of me, leaving me wanting so much more with her. I could tell she was unhappy in her marriage. Her husband, Maestro Radcliffe, paraded her around like some vacuous little doll. She was supposed to look perfect at all times, not one hair out of place, speak only when spoken to, and generally mind her own business. She truly was a bird in a gilded cage."

I lean forward, listening raptly to the old man's story. I don't know where he's headed, but by the sound of things, he might not be too shocked by one of my romances after all.

"The night of my premier with the New York Philharmonic, playing Rachmaninoff's Piano Concerto Number Two in C minor, she showed up to my dressing room after the performance ended. I had just finished speaking to patrons and signing their programs. It was Christmas, and I'll never forget how she stood in the doorway of my dressing room, where a silly sprig of mistletoe hung. I begrudgingly kissed her. It was the boldest move I'd ever committed up to that point. After the kiss, we stood silently, drinking each other in with our eyes, and I told her, 'Divorce Maestro Radcliffe and wait one year. I'll come to you then.'"

He pauses, taking a deep breath before continuing, "After that day, we corresponded through letters that grew increasingly scandalous as her address changed from NYC to Reno, Nevada, and she established residency to divorce the authoritative conductor. But her husband didn't go away quietly. One year later, he showed up at our intimate elopement to confront us. The scene culminated in a vicious fistfight between me and the much older man. I broke both hands during it, and the ring finger on my right hand never worked quite as well as before. Of course, I managed other ways to compensate for the weakened digit. But that's how I won a wife and lost a solo career on the East Coast. Fortunately, the West Coast proved more welcoming and tolerant of scandals...and mildly impaired fingers."

"Oh, my goodness, Mr. Horowitz, that's quite a romance

story. It could stand alongside any of my books. Did you have any children together?"

"One daughter," he says, suddenly fascinated by the blankets draped over his lap.

"Does she live near the hospital? Does she visit?"

He shrugs. "She lives in Sacramento, just an hour from here. But we had a falling out a few years before Gracie's death because I didn't want to put my wife in a nursing home, and my daughter wouldn't listen to me. So, I'm sorry to say I haven't spoken to her since."

"Oh no," I say, covering my mouth with my hand. "Does she even know you're sick and in the hospital?"

He shrugs. "I doubt she'd care."

"I can't believe that for one minute. She's your daughter."

He looks exhausted as he counters, "Too much water under that bridge."

"But it's Christmas, Mr. Horowitz."

"You'd be surprised. But enough about me. Back to you and Dr. Knight. You have to admit this particular setup by fate is pretty damn good. I mean, it would make for a great romance novel. Wouldn't it?"

"That depends on a lot of unknown factors. Like whether we're even each other's type..."

"Honey, you'd have to be blind not to notice how he looks at you."

I twist the corners of my mouth up. "Maybe, but with him on the rebound and me still sorting out Reggie's mess, I don't think it's a good mix... Now, back to your daughter. You at least need to call her to explain what's going on."

The man looks defiant. "I don't have to do anything of the sort."

"Yes, you do," I reply firmly, crossing my arms. "If you're going to make me go out with a total stranger, then the least you can do is accept my stipulation in return. If you want me to go on a revenge date with Dr. Knight, you must call your daughter and speak to her. Even if it's only for a few minutes."

"But my personal life has nothing to do with the romance we're trying to write for you," he counters.

"It has everything to do with it, actually. If this whole scenario were a romance I was writing, there would definitely be room for a heartwarming family reunion."

He crosses his arms over his chest, looking grim. "You really do drive a hard bargain, don't you?"

I nod, offering, "If it helps, I'll call her myself and then hand the phone to you."

"No, I'll make the call. I'll do it. But only after you and Fletcher go out on your hospital date."

I shake my head, chuckling. "You know you drive a hard bargain, too, and you've probably heard this before, but you're as stubborn as a mule."

He laughs. "You have to be stubborn to make it in classical music as a pianist. Stubborn and stupid, and God gave me extra of both. Do you know how to make phones play music?"

I nod.

"Would you put on a piece for me, in that case?"

"Certainly. What is it?"

"The 1967 recording of Rachmaninoff's Second Concerto by the New York Philharmonic under the direction of Maestro Radcliffe."

Sure enough, when I type in those parameters, the recording comes up. Putting the phone on speaker and turning the volume all the way up, I ask, "Are you ready to hear yourself play?"

He shrugs. "I've never been a huge fan of listening to my own recordings. But this piece is dripping with romance. I think you could use a dose of it before your date tonight."

"You are incorrigible, Mr. Horowitz," I laugh as I press play, and the piano comes in dark and passionate, shadowed by the string orchestra. The recording must be remastered because the instruments sound lush and rich, and the melody curls around me as I listen, settling back into the uncomfortable hospital chair.

The old man closes his eyes, and his fingers reflexively move with the recording, his face somehow transfigured into a younger, more vibrant version of himself. Watching him, I decide no matter what, I'll find a way for him to talk with his daughter again...even if it's only for a few moments to acknowledge the holiday and his health concerns.

As the recording continues, I pinch myself thinking that the man seated in front of me performed this, and I wonder if this was the night that he and Gracie kissed under the mistletoe for the first time. About midway through the first movement, tears fill my eyes as the passion of the piece swells into a gorgeous Slavic theme, and I wipe my cheeks, still watching enraptured as the frail little old man's fingers move lithely with the melody and harmony.

Somehow, despite everything that's happened between Reggie and me, I don't feel depressed. Instead, I focus on the music and this intimate little moment with a true musical great.

Suddenly, his eyes open in the middle of a solo between the piano and the cello, and he asks, "Honey, why are you crying?"

"Because this music is so beautiful. I can't believe you're sharing this with me, and I barely know you."

He smiles, "If there's one thing I could tell you and make you understand, it would be this. Time flies so much faster than you realize. In the blink of an eye, you'll end up like me... in a hospital bed, reflecting back on everything rather than looking forward. And that's why I don't want you or Dr. Knight to waste any more time on the wrong people. You may not be right for each other, but if you can make each other's holidays a little better, why not?"

"You know, the same goes for you," I reply, wiping away more tears as the second movement starts, enveloping the room in more sensual, rich sounds. "Your daughter will always be family no matter what. Even if all you get are a few minutes on the phone to say 'I love you,' don't you think it would be worth it?"

For the first time since meeting Mr. Horowitz, he looks teary-eyed. "Alright, alright. I thought I was the most stubborn bastard in this hospital. But you're rather obstinate yourself, although certainly no bastard."

"I'll take that as a compliment. We're both going outside of our comfort zones tonight, and we're doing it in the name of Gracie and the mistletoe kiss."

He smiles thinly, leaning forward to seize my hand and squeeze it.

Chapter Six

FLETCHER

After stopping by the break room to ensure I look presentable, I enter four thirty-five to the sounds of classical music. The Rachmaninoff. Mr. Horowitz plays this piece often.

"Regaling Ms. O'Day with one of your hits, I see," I deliver in a grumpy voice, smiling despite myself.

Tears pour down Drew's lovely dark complexion, filling me with instant apprehension. Is she crying over Reggie and everything that she learned today? It wouldn't surprise me. After all, I would be a lot more broken up about Mandy if it wasn't for the fact I've lived this painful pattern for five years and am, quite frankly, over it. And I have a lovely new woman to look forward to getting to know. *If* she can quit crying over her ex.

"If I came back at a bad time, I'll go. We can always do the whole revenge date thing another time…or not at all."

She laughs, letting go of Mr. Horowitz's hand and wiping both cheeks. "No, this is as good a time as any. As long as Mr. Horowitz keeps regaling me with his music and stories of his past and life with Gracie, I'm going to cry. But I'm also hungry and could use something a little less emotional to focus on."

I make a mental note to keep things light. "Alright then. Mr. Horowitz, I'm stealing your new girl for a bit. I hope you won't mind."

He smiles. "You two, go and have fun. As much fun as can be had on a revenge date, that is."

I offer the black-haired beauty my arm, and she takes it with a smile. I savor the faint smell of sandalwood and jasmine that envelops me at this close range, feeling sparks light up where our arms and sides touch. Covering her hand with mine, I let out a long sigh, strangely mesmerized by her touch. My cock stirs, and I'm glad my scrubs aren't tight-fitting.

"May I call you Drew?" I ask, and she laughs, shaking her head.

"Are you always this old-fashioned acting, or is Mr. Horowitz rubbing off on you?"

"The old guy does have a way of influencing people, doesn't he?"

"Yes, that's true."

"So, where are we off to on our revenge date, Drew? The cafeteria or Starbucks for more egg bites?"

She laughs again, and I wonder if she genuinely finds me funny or if she's nervous. Mandy hardly ever laughed at any of my jokes, which turned me into a bitter, grumpy man over time. But I'd try again for Drew, especially with little victories like this.

"Tell me what delights we might enjoy in the cafeteria."

"Okay, they do this amazing sourdough bread bowl filled with clam chowder or broccoli and cheese soup, which is shockingly good for cafeteria food. And they also have a breakfast burrito that my staff claim is to die for, although I have yet to try it."

"I'm on keto, so maybe we should stick to egg bites."

"Why are you on keto, if I might ask?"

"Because there's a little too much junk in the trunk, if you know what I mean."

I shake my head. "No, I don't know what you mean. I don't want to objectify you or anything, but you're stunning... better than perfect just the way you are."

"You think so?" she asks in that silky smooth voice that I could get used to hearing a lot more of.

I'd worship the shit out of her body, if she were mine. But that's not really the right thing to say under the circumstances. So, instead, I answer, "Yes, I do, and I know so, too."

"Reggie always told me I was overweight...that I needed to slim down if I wanted to be with him."

"Reggie's an idiot," I reply, frowning. "And I'm not just saying that because he and Mandy appear to be together."

"I may regret asking this, but what's Mandy like?"

I grimace. "Do you mean like in the looks department or personality-wise?"

"All of the above."

I cock my head to the side, searching for the right words. "For starters, she would never wander into an old guy's room like you and spend hours keeping him company. I haven't seen him look this revitalized in weeks. It's amazing what a little TLC and a feminine touch can do for a guy like that."

"Well, he's an amazing man. I have half a mind to write a book about him after the life story he told me—"

"You're a writer?"

She smiles broadly, "Yes. My romance pen name is Drew Devereaux, and one of my books is being turned into a movie. You might have seen the trailer for *Ice and Heat?*"

"No, ma'am. It sounds intriguing, though. You'll have to tell me more about it after we fill up our trays."

"You brought me to the cafeteria, after all? I thought I told you I was on keto."

"Go back on keto tomorrow, if you like. But right now, please eat and enjoy yourself free from Reggie's judgment. Isn't that the whole gist of a revenge date, after all?"

"I like the way you think, Dr. Knight."

"Please call me Fletcher."

"Alright then, Fletcher," she says with a faint smile, grabbing a cafeteria tray.

After we load up on soup bowls and salt and pepper packets, I pay for everything. We avoid the small crowd in the middle of the dining room, sitting next to a window where we can look out at the piling white sheets of snow.

"It looks like I'm going to be stuck here all night," she observes quietly, resting her chin on her hand as she looks out the window. Bringing my hand up, I push a stray hair off her beautiful dark pink cheek, and she smiles, taking my hand and pressing it against her face.

"Your hands are so big and warm, Fletcher."

I stroke her cheek with my thumb, swallowing hard. "They're nimble, too."

Her eyes widen, and I instantly kick myself for the stupid comment. "I meant in the sense that I'm a good doctor. I perform intricate medical procedures with them."

"I'm sure you do," she says in a voice like dark honey. "What other talents do you have?"

I laugh, sitting back and pulling at my pants legs to give myself more room. "Well, I'm decent at darts and pretty damn good at open heart surgery."

"I imagine that comes in handy in a place like this." She chuckles.

I nod.

"I'm also skilled at in-flight interventions, thanks to the

military, although they never let me on a bird around here, despite the fact my brother, Hawk, flies for the hospital."

"So, they keep you grounded?"

"Unfortunately. Apparently, I deliver much greater value on the ground than in the air. Let's see...what else? I'm an okay singer at the karaoke bar. Mostly country music and an average equestrian, too. My brothers would be the first to tell you I'm not the fastest or the showiest. Those titles would go to Christian, Hawk, Zane, or Flynn. But I know how to cut a herd and wrestle a steer, for what that's worth."

"You're a man of many talents. So, how many brothers do you have?"

"Fifteen."

Her eyes round, and she sits back, her brows knitting. "Are you Mormon, Catholic, or something?"

I laugh. "No, I grew up in a foster home at Rough & Ready Ranch in Hollister."

"Oh, I see. What happened to your biological parents?"

"Who the hell knows?" I say, shaking my head. "The official story is that they both ended up in prison at the same time, and none of my immediate relatives wanted me. I don't blame them. I was a true hellion, but nothing the Army couldn't eventually straighten out."

"That doesn't sound like the story of an esteemed cardiologist to me," she replies, side-eyeing me curiously. I long to reach out, touch her soft, cocoa-colored skin, and run my thumb across her full lower lip. My cock stirs as I wonder what she tastes like before catching myself and clearing my throat. My heart pounds against my ribs.

"How do you know I'm an esteemed cardiologist?"

"Mr. Horowitz made me look it up."

"Ever the matchmaker, I see."

She smiles broadly. "But you are very well-recognized in your field. Why not tell me that side of your story?"

39

I shrug. "I can't imagine you'd want to hear much about it. Mandy often accused me of bragging and being a narcissist, you know, taking all the attention for myself. So, I guess I'm trying to turn over a new leaf."

She licks her lips, looking at the tabletop pensively for a moment. When her golden brown eyes find mine again, sparks zing between our pupils as she says, "Have you ever noticed how some people will accuse you of what they're guilty of?"

I look up to my right, thinking about her observation for a moment. "You may be on to something there."

"Yeah, like Reggie. He always accused me of lying and cheating on him, even though I think you know enough about my ex to realize those were his problems, not mine."

"How long were you two together?" I ask.

"Two years."

"And how old are you, Drew, if you don't mind my asking?"

She wets her lower lip with her bubblegum-pink tongue. "Thirty-two. And you?"

"Thirty-four."

She nods.

"Why do you think you stayed with Reggie for two years? I stayed with Mandy for five, by the way, so no judgment."

She purses her lips tightly together, looking up for a moment before leveling her gaze on me and answering, "I guess the relationship came with a certain comfort level. And we had enough in common to keep things going. You know, we were both outgoing and liked hip hop and electronic music. We liked dressing up to the nines and going out dancing, that kind of stuff. But the more I look back on our relationship now, the more I realize it was really, really fundamentally immature. What about you and Mandy?"

"Well, she was everything I thought I was looking for on paper. A good-looking blonde in the medical field with shared interests like horseback riding and country music. We did a lot of karaoke and line dancing together. You know, that kind of stuff."

"Have you ever dated a sister before?" Drew asks, raising her eyebrows.

"No, ma'am. Have you ever dated a white guy?"

She smiles faintly. "No."

"I must say, even though you haven't asked, I've never found a woman more beautiful or alluring in my entire life than you are. Are you what I'd usually class as my type? No. But I've been wrong about plenty in my life, and I'm not afraid to admit it here, too." I stop, shaking my head, feeling my heart expand with warmth as I look at her. "There's something about you that...I don't know..."

"I think you know. Just say it."

"I don't want to sound too forward, but something about you draws me in, makes me want to touch you and protect you simultaneously. I don't know what it is."

"You should touch me then and find out." Her words make me freeze. *Did I hear her right?* My mouth quirks up into a lopsided grin, and I reach out to stroke her left hand, resting on the tabletop. My fingertips feather over hers lightly as chemistry zings between us, and I let out a sharp exhale, resting my hand over hers and continuing to caress her with my fingertips.

"Well?" she says quietly.

"There's an awful lot of chemistry bouncing back and forth between us, don't you think?"

She smiles. "It's undeniable. Does that intimidate you, Fletcher?"

"I spent fourteen years in the Army, and cardiology isn't a job for the weak-kneed, so there's not much that intimidates me. But if you're looking for a confession, I must say you being a romance writer makes me feel a little nervous."

"And why is that?" she asks, letting her fingers dance over my palm and sending delicious shivers of desire coursing up my arm and straight to my heart.

"Because you basically specialize in romance. How could I ever begin to live up to those kinds of expectations?"

Chapter Seven

DREW

"One beat at a time," I answer, letting my fingers tangle with the handsome physician's atop the table. My heart pounds in my chest, and I cross my legs tightly, trying to put a stop to the pulsing at the juncture between my legs.

Inviting this guy to touch me is the worst mistake I could ever make because the sparks flying between us are unreal. With a naughty smile, I wonder what he could do to the rest of my body.

"One beat at a time. I know what that means as a cardiologist. But what do *you* mean?" he asks in a low, raw tone, swallowing loudly as his eyes flicker to our entwined hands.

"The best romance novels all follow the same basic premise or structure. The structure is made up of beats, each representing a critical step in the couple's growth as partners. For example, the first beat is the meet-cute, where the two main characters come together for the first time."

"And how does our meet-cute rank in your expert knowledge?"

"Two main characters with the same back-to-back orders

squabbling over who gets what? I'd use it in a story. Especially if one of those parties were a drop-dead gorgeous cardiologist."

He smiles, his cheeks flushing. "Well, it would only really work with a stunning romance writer to counter him, don't you think?"

I smile, letting go of his hand and putting mine under the table. He follows, claiming my fingers beneath the table and tangling them with his while he continues to caress me.

"What about the second beat, Drew? Have we reached it yet?"

I nod. "There was a 'no way' thrown in there when you argued with me over whose order was whose, even though we ordered the exact same things."

"Oh, yeah?" he says, raising an eyebrow. "Well, I wanted my order, and that was that. Simple."

"Are you always that much of a pain in the ass when it comes to things that don't really matter?"

"But they do matter," he says firmly. "I didn't want your order any more than you wanted mine."

I counter, "But they were the same." My hand comes to a stop and starts to pull away from his.

"Okay, okay," he says quietly. "You win that round. Now, give me back your hand," he growls in a rich tone that makes my pussy throb some more. I don't know what this man has done to my lady parts, but they're definitely out of control.

"I'll admit I can be a little neurotic at times. It stems from years in the military and what I do for a living. There's no margin for error when it comes to heart surgery. And there's only one right way most of the time."

"Fair enough. But I'm not sure I can put up with some-body so grouchy or neurotic."

"And I'm not sure I can handle a gal who thinks stealing other people's orders is okay."

I laugh, shaking my head and making my curls bob. "Touché."

"What beat comes next, Drew?"

"Adhesion."

"Adhesion?" His handsome face flushes, and his eyebrows furrow. "What does that involve?"

"Circumstances where the two main characters are thrown together by fate, forcing them to get to know each other and fall in love."

"Is that about where you think we are?"

I purse my lips, shaking my head. "I don't know. We couldn't be more opposites. You know, I'm a SoCal girl into hip hop and nightclubs. You're a country doctor with a confessed love for karaoke and line dancing."

He leans forward, pulling my hand onto his powerful, muscular thigh so that he can softly stroke the skin on the back of my forearm. "I think you'd kick ass at karaoke, but that's just me guessing. And you in a tight-fitting pair of Ariats with cowboy boots shaking your ass. Well, I could get behind that sight."

"So, wait, I didn't even think this through. Are you telling me you normally walk around in Wranglers and boots?"

The corners of his mouth turn down slightly. "Is there a problem with that?"

"And a cowboy hat and a belt buckle?"

"Of course, ma'am."

"I've never really been into cowboys."

"Just think how many horses you could save," he says, flashing me a gorgeous grin with big, white, straight teeth.

"That's never been high on my priority list." I laugh.

"See, I have a theory about that. A little more time spent with me, and I bet I could put it at the top of your priority list."

"You don't seem to lack confidence," I reply.

"Not when it comes to what I'm good at. But you'd have to get over your dumbass ex-boyfriend and open your mind up to new and different experiences."

I add, "Well, that's a two-way street, you know. I'd expect you to open your mind and try new stuff, too. Including clubbing and listening to hip hop."

"Drew, I was in the Army for fourteen years. I challenge you to name a hip hop song I don't know the lyrics to... Outkast 'So fresh, So clean,' Ludacris 'Southern Hospitality,' Nelly 'Country Grammar.' I may listen to country, but that doesn't preclude me from enjoying hip hop, rock, and even electronic music. And I did plenty of clubbing overseas, too."

"Alright, not bad. So you can dance to electronic music?"

"Hell, yeah, and it doesn't have to be in a straight line."

"You sound like a lot of fun," I admit. "Why would a girl like Mandy let you go?"

"The same reason a guy like Reggie would fuck things up with you. They wouldn't recognize a good thing if it bit them on the ass. Now, though, they get to find out what a bad thing looks like, thanks to each other."

I nod, frowning. "You know what's going to happen next, right?"

He shrugs, eyeing me.

"They're both going to come crawling back to us, begging for a second chance."

"Mandy and I are well past second chances. I've never felt more sure about moving on than I do now. But where are you at with Reggie? Honestly, Drew. I don't want you to sugarcoat it or anything."

"Very much enjoying our revenge date, to be honest, and maybe looking for something more..."

"Like?"

"What are your thoughts when it comes to revenge sex?"

Fletcher sits back, letting out a long sigh, his eyes molten as they meet mine. "I don't know about any of that. But I do know I'd like to get to know you better. Much better. And it would have nothing to do with Mandy or Reggie."

"Alright, then," I say quietly, smiling at him. "And what does getting to know me better look like?"

"We better eat some of our soup before it gets cold, and then I'll show you."

We eat in silence, catching each other's eyes now and again. My heart pounds behind my ribs as I watch him lick his spoon clean of a bite of broccoli cheese soup, twirling it on his tongue. He lets out a satisfied groan that makes my whole body quiver with want.

His eyes round when I return the favor, licking my eating utensil clean. His tongue darts out over his generous, kissable lips as his eyes meet mine, coursing with a yearning I've never seen in a man's gaze before. It puts every nerve in my body on high alert and sends anticipatory flames licking and incinerating their way through my body.

Staring at his gorgeous mouth, I wonder what the handsome doctor tastes like and what his tongue would feel like on my lips and my nipples and regions much lower and naughtier. I squeeze my legs tightly together beneath the table, chiding myself to take it down a notch. But that's a tall order with this rugged, giant of a man sitting on the opposite side of the table from me, searing me with his hungry gaze.

Chapter Eight

A fter we eat as much as we can and throw the rest away, he grabs my hand, leading me down the hallway with him. Looking at his watch, he says, "I only have about twenty minutes left on my dinner break. But I heard there's this thing going on tonight that you might like, seeing as you seem to love music."

"I do."

He leads me down a long corridor that opens up to a gigantic waiting room with large windows looking out onto the snowy landscape. A live string quartet dressed in black plays holiday music next to a massive Christmas tree, reaching up into the vaulted ceiling of the second story. The dimly lit area glitters with the white and blue lights of the tree. Fletcher grabs my hands, drawing me towards him to dance.

"But we're the only people dancing," I whisper nervously as he wraps his arm around my waist, drawing me close.

"I don't care what other people are doing, Drew. I want to know more about you. Tell me what your childhood was like. What kinds of friends you had. What you dreamed of doing when you grew up." He snuggles me against his hard chest, resting his chin on my head. He smells like a spiced forest, rugged and fresh, and I can hear his heart beating in his chest as we slowly move around the dance floor.

"Reggie would never do anything like this with me. He'd be way too worried about what other people think."

"Too worried about what other people think, but not worried enough about what you think."

"Exactly," I nod, feeling his scrubs rub on my cheek. "Oops!" I say, pulling back. "I think I just got some of my makeup on your uniform," I say, pointing at a dark blush spot on the front of his light blue shirt.

"Sexy, I don't mean to sound crass, but I'd like a lot more than your makeup on me."

"But everyone'll see..."

"See what? That I've got more going on in my life for once than being a lonely ass fool? Well, I'm okay with that." He pulls me back tightly against him, encircling me in his large, warm arms. "Mandy would've never been down for anything like this, either. But the more I think about it, I don't know if she ever really loved me or even enjoyed being around me. I was more of a commodity to her. I crossed off just enough boxes that she was hellbent on keeping me while still keeping her distance from me. It was a lonely way to conduct a relationship, and I don't want to do that anymore."

"Yeah, Reggie only wanted me around when it fit his schedule. He'd have been so mad if I accidentally got makeup on his clothes. Looking back on it now, I have to admit it's because a mark like that would've given him away to the other women he was seeing on the side. Or maybe I was on the side. I don't even know how that works. Was I his main girl or side chick? God, that question makes me feel like a loser."

"You're too damn good for him. That's all you need to know, Drew."

We dance in silence for a while, and I nestle into his

warmth and strength, feeling oddly at home. Almost as if I were meant to be here with him like this.

"Why do you think you settled for a guy like Reggie?" Fletcher asks, sending the sound of his voice rumbling through my core.

I shake my head against his chest, absorbed in the sound of his strong heartbeat. "I guess because he had a fun personality and a decent sense of humor. And I liked how outgoing he was, even though we ended up competing with each other over time."

"It was the opposite for Mandy and me. We're both fairly private, quiet people. So, conversation ran out quickly between us. We also prized our alone time so much that it was inevitable we would grow apart. I imagine the perfect match would be an outgoing partner with a more reserved one. Take us, for example. I could sit here and listen to you talk for hours, and I'd be happy to let you dazzle and be the bright, extroverted one at any parties we went to together. In fact, it would relieve me to relax and let you work the crowd and make everyone fall in love with you the way..."

"The way?" I ask, my voice trembling, unsure whether I'm ready to hear him verbalize the overwhelming emotions swirling between us.

"Nothing. I'm getting carried away."

We dance silently, holding each other even closer now, a strange sort of urgency building between us. The intensity of the moment puts a thick lump of desire in my throat, and I want him so badly that I can taste it.

Clearing my throat, I look up at him, remarking, "It would be nice to have a man who appreciates my personality rather than feels threatened by it...and who I don't have to chase down every fifteen minutes with a new woman that he decides to be outgoing with."

"We are opposites in about every imaginable way possible.

But dare I say, it feels more like we're complements. Like we could fill in the strengths and interests of the other person. You know, complete each other...although I don't mean to get all *Jerry Maguire* on you."

I chuckle, "Hey, I love *Jerry Maguire*. That's one of my favorite movies, and it does a good job with the romantic beats we were talking about earlier."

"And what beat would this be?" he asks, leaning down so close to me that I can feel the heat from his breath on the shell of my ear. The sensation sends delicious shivers of desire rippling through my core.

"Well, 'no way two' was when we started talking about being opposites and discussing whether or not we could make it work considering our interests, and then the 'inkling it could work' kind of came after that when you put two and two together about our opposite characteristics complementing each other. So, I'd say we're firmly in 'deepening desire' territory."

He pulls me more tightly against his core until I can feel his long, thick arousal pressed against my stomach. I swallow hard, pulling him just as tightly against me with my arms around his waist. If I could get away with it, I would grab his athletic ass, too.

"I couldn't agree with you more," he says in a deep growl. "So, what's next if I might ask you to forecast a little."

My cheeks burn as I stare into his sizzling, indigo eyes. "It's different for every author, but for me, I'd probably throw in a super hot sex scene right about now."

Fletcher smiles, his face drawing closer to mine. "How about we start with a mind-blowing kiss?"

His lips cover mine gently, tentatively, before gaining urgency. He deepens the angle, demanding more from me. My arms leave his waist, wrapping around his neck and drawing him closer as he moans softly against my mouth, causing delicious vibrations to scuttle through me. My lips part with a sigh, and his hot, soft tongue sweeps into my mouth, claiming me with a deep-throated, feral sound that tightens the tension between my legs to the point of pain.

Suddenly, he pulls back, his face flushed. Clearing his throat, he says, "I can't do this at work, or I'll have to put on a lab coat. But fuck, Drew, you taste amazing, and you feel so good in my arms. I don't know how to describe what's happening other than we feel like we fit together."

I nod, desire lodged in my throat. "The chemistry flying between us is insane. But even crazier is the strange sense of comfortableness I feel with you. Almost like we already know each other somehow. I don't know what it means, but I don't want it to end."

"Neither do I," he says, leaning down for another kiss. "I've got something else to show you before break ends." He leads me down a long corridor that connects with a walkway high in the air. Enclosed in glass, it affords incredible views of the sky and surrounding landscape. When he turns off the lights, we can see the snowy blizzard twirling and tumbling around us.

I crane my neck, looking up as he comes up behind me, wrapping his arms around me. I settle back into him with a satisfied sigh. Somehow, our bodies mesh perfectly, his big and hard, mine soft and curvy, complementing each other like our personalities.

Resting his chin atop my head again, he says, "When it's not blizzarding outside, and you come down this hallway after dark, on clear nights, it affords amazing views of the stars. I'd love to show it to you sometime...when the weather's nicer."

"It's beautiful with the snow like this..." I say. As much as I'd love to believe there could be a future between us and that I might stand in this walkway with him someday, staring up at the stars, I catch myself. The last thing I need is to dive head-first into another long-distance relationship. After all, they have never worked out for me, and all my boyfriends have cheated. A part of me wonders how many women Dr. Knight has brought down this same hallway to romance.

But I push the errant thought away, adding, "I bet it's stunning on a starry night, too." My breath catches in my throat, tight with want.

"Not as stunning as you," he says, turning me towards him to taste my lips again. My heart sings at the feel of him against me, even as another part of me holds back, trying to shield myself from more heartbreak.

How could a man as good-looking and romantic as Dr. Fletcher Knight be anything but a player? No matter what he says about his past relationship with Mandy or what he leaves out. It's simply not possible. Nevertheless, it's also none of my business. Instead, I focus on the feel and taste of his excruciatingly soft, skilled mouth as he claims me until I lean against him, trying to catch my breath.

"I'm glad we listened to the old guy," he says, panting, too. "Because this is the best night of my entire life."

"Really?" I manage, my heart thumping against my ribs.

"Yes. Because you actually want to be with me, Drew. I can feel that difference. You're generous and giving. You listen to me and pay attention to what I'm saying. It sounds kind of pathetic, but I'm not used to that. And I don't want this night to end. So, after my shift, will you consider coming back to my ski lodge with me? It's just up the road. I don't have any expectations about what will happen between us. But I need to spend more time with you and get to know you better. I want to know everything about you, so the next time I ask you to tell me about yourself, I won't let you sidetrack me by bringing up Reggie. You think you can deal with that?"

I smile, palming his chest where I left my makeup stain

earlier. "I'm not the kind of girl who goes home with random men."

"Sexy, can you really call me a random man? Besides, I swear I'll be on my best behavior. Scout's honor."

"I'm more worried about me being on my best behavior."

He chuckles deep in his throat. "I can't make any guarantees for you, and I wouldn't want to. After all, you did make that earlier revenge sex comment."

"I did, didn't I?" I ask in a low voice, palming his hard chest. "I don't even know what I'm thinking right now. But yes, I'll go to your ski lodge with you. Just to get to know you better...without expectations."

"Good," he says, holding me tightly. "And on the bright side, it'll be much more comfortable than sleeping in Mr Horowitz's room on the couch tonight. Or, God forbid, in your car in the parking lot."

I shiver in his arms just thinking about it. He draws me closer, warming my heart and body and flooding me with the same dangerous desire that's threatened to overtake me since meeting the muscular cardiologist.

Chapter Nine

D rew's eyebrows jump into her hairline when I show up at Mr. Horowitz's room wearing my Wranglers, boots, buckle, button-down flannel shirt, Carhartt coat, and black Stetson at the end of my shift. My patient snores softly, the lights low in his room. So, I lead her outside before saying anything. "Alright, lay it on me."

She eyes me up and down for a moment, her cheeks darkening. "Old Town Road meets plain old sexy."

"Oh yeah?" I ask, wrapping my arm possessively around her waist. "Is that the only jacket you brought?" I eye her puffy purple jacket.

"Yes, is there a problem?"

"Sexy, it's in the single digits outside. You're going to freeze your gorgeous ass off. Let's go by the break room to grab one of my extra jackets out of my locker."

Desire lodges in my throat the closer we get to the break room, which turns up empty as usual. Finally being alone in a room with Drew does crazy shit to my head and my heart. My thoughts swirl, and my pulse pounds against my ribcage as I close the door behind us, hearing the distant strains of CNN in the background.

All I need is for her to look down or keep her distance from me. It's all I need to stay remotely decent. Instead, the stunning ebony woman turns to face me, stepping so close I can smell desire mixed with her sandalwood and jasmine perfume.

Her dark eyes are two molten pools of lust, and her alluring tongue flicks across her generous lips, setting my body on fire and making my cock rock hard.

Clearing my throat, I say what's painfully obvious, "There's rarely anyone in here..."

"Oh yeah?" She says, arching her eyebrow. Electricity crackles in the air between us as my hand reaches for her face, and I rub my thumb across her smooth, soft cheek.

She states more of the obvious. "I kind of like the idea of finally being alone with you."

"I more than kind of like it," I confess, bringing my hand to the back of her neck and drawing closer until our lips are inches apart.

If this were any other woman. Hell, if it were Mandy, I would never even entertain the thoughts rolling through my mind right now. But I need Drew in a visceral way...body and soul.

Under any other circumstances, I could control these feelings. I'm a master of self-denial as a former military man and thoroughly trained doctor. I could press into my willpower and stay gentlemanly if she wasn't looking at me like this, her eyes pooling with need, her nostrils flaring, and her lips trembling for my touch.

"I'm over Mandy. Like way over her. But where are you at with Reggie?" I whisper, trying to hang onto logic and reason and losing the battle as I draw closer, so close that I can feel her hot breath against my lips.

"Reggie who?" She says breathlessly, removing my cowboy hat and setting it on the break room table.

CNN evaporates into the background as I crash into her mouth and body, the hiss of our heated breathing overtaking the room. The rustle of our clothes sounds as she palms my back frantically, running her hands lower with each pass until she grips my firm ass in both her hands. "I could get used to your extroversion," I say with a dark laugh, my hands squeezing her waist and hips and pulling her demandingly against me.

"The coat," she says, pulling her full, delicious lips from mine. "We're here for your coat."

"Yes, we are," I say, knowing there's reason in her words. But my hands keep exploring her soft, curvy body, falling in love with every dip and plane of her and wanting so much more. "Do you want the coat, or do you want a little more privacy first?"

"A little more privacy," she gasps without hesitation, and I walk with her in my arms, leading her backward towards the rooms where nurses and doctors sometimes take naps. None of the doors lock, and all open outward except for one. That's where I navigate her, desperate to avoid interruptions.

We barely make it through the door, and I have her pressed against the wall, letting my hard core sink into her inviting softness. "You feel so good, Drew. So fucking enticing. I can't help myself. You really need to stop me, you know."

"Do I need to? Well, then, who's going to stop me, cowboy?"

"Fuck, sexy..." I shouldn't do this, but I can't help myself. My hand drops to her black slacks, feeling her mound through the fabric of her pants. I rub her with increasing intensity, watching her eyes ignite as I give her the friction she needs.

"I've never wanted a woman so much in my entire life," I confess in raw tones, and she nods her consent. My hand unbuttons her waistband before I hear the inviting hiss of her zipper, feeling my cock throb with something approaching anguish. But he's not getting in on this action. I'll only let this go so far, even though we've already far exceeded my original coat-retrieving intentions.

My hand slides down the front of her silky underwear, and she lets out a tiny whimper, and then another as my fingers greedily push her panties to the side, searching for her heat.

"I'm sorry I'm wearing granny panties," she apologizes. "I didn't know I'd have a..." She lets out a satisfied sigh as I find her wet folds. "A...sexy cowboy in my drawers."

I groan frantically, letting my thumb and fingers swipe through her honeyed folds. I fucking love the warm flood that greets me.

"You're so wet," I whisper, pressing her harder into the wall as my fingers tease the entrance to her pussy. She's clean-shaven and smooth, and I fight with my last remaining fibers of control not to drop down onto my knees, throw her leg over my shoulder, and dive into her pussy with my face. But I need to keep my foot securely over the edge of the door in case a colleague decides to enter the break room and try this door.

"And your fingers *are* nimble, Dr. Knight...*very nimble*," she purrs.

"That's not all that's nimble on me, sexy. I'm going to eat you out so good, woman. You won't be able to talk. You'll fucking struggle to breathe. I won't stop until you cover me in your cum."

"Dr. Knight," she gasps, melting into me some more. I find the rough spot near the front of her slick, juicy channel, stroking it and curving my finger back towards me. A long, chest-deep sigh escapes her lips, and I know I've found what my girl needs.

Jamming my left foot and leg against the door even harder, I get my other hand in the mix, running my thumb through her dripping folds. Then, I find the nub at the top of her pussy lips, rubbing it with my arousal-slick thumb until it swells and hardens. The breath hisses from her throat.

"I know my anatomy, too…"

"Yes, you do…" She exhales sharply, her head rolling back against the wall, her eyes closed, and little involuntary moans escaping her lips.

Suddenly, I hear the door in the break room slam behind someone who's walked in, and the TV volume increases. I hear the Keurig water heating up, staring down at Drew, who's so close to coming, I can see ecstasy written all over her face. Her eyes plead with mine for what to do, and I answer by bringing my mouth down hard over hers and picking up the pace of my fingers.

Her arms wrap around my back, clinging to the fabric of my shirt as she surrenders to me, drenching my hand. She screams her release into my mouth, and I do the best I can to mute it with my tongue and lips, feeling like I could fucking conquer the world. No woman has ever given herself so entirely to me. I fucking adore it.

The doorknob by my hip turns, and I jam my leg hard against the wood to keep whoever's messing with it from pushing it open. Drew's face is filled with silent panic as I reluctantly release her lips, turning towards the entrance and grumbling, "Somebody's in here."

"Oh, sorry, Dr. Knight," an oblivious female voice calls out. It's Molly. "You've left your cowboy hat on the break room table."

Swallowing hard and trying not to sound like I'm panting, I call back, "Thank you. I'll grab it before I leave." An excruciatingly awkward silence follows.

We stand frozen until the footsteps retreat, and the break room door opens and shuts again. Drew's lips draw a thin line, holding back nervous giggles until the coast is clear. I let out a long, relieved sigh, chuckling with her under my breath. "That was a close one, sexy. But well worth every nail-biting moment."

Pulling my hands out of her pants, I lick my fingers clean, savoring every drop of her musky, tangy flavor. Her jaw goes slack as she watches, and I chuckle deep in my throat. "You taste like my new addiction, sexy."

"Do I?" she says, her breathing still strained and her hand clutching her chest.

I seize her in my arms, kissing her with a newfound intensity. The kind of intensity that doesn't just want to claim her. Now, I need to keep her.

"How many other girls have you done this with...in this room?" she asks, and I can sense she's trying to get her head screwed back on straight.

Her question makes me laugh. She still doesn't get what kind of man I am. "I've never done what we just did in any hospital with any woman ever. Let alone in this room."

"Not even Mandy?" she inquires suspiciously.

"Hell no," I laugh. "I'll spare you the fucking details, but Mandy never responded to me the way you do, Drew. I fucking love it. I can't get enough of your body and the way you want me." My voice trembles at the end, catching me off guard and making me feel like a wimp. But her eyes warm as recognition floods her expression, inspired by my obvious sincerity.

"Good," she says, a seductive smile capturing her lips. "For the record, I've never done what we just did with any man, either. This was a total first for me. A forbidden workplace first, and I loved every second of it."

I run my hand through my hair, smiling. "So, you might be into cowboys after all?"

She licks her lips slowly, igniting my entire body on fire

again. I can't take much more of this. I need her so badly. "Actually, I think I'm into you, Dr. Knight."

No woman has ever made me feel so wanted or needed…or so passionate. I didn't know such feelings were possible. Whatever romantic magic the writer's weaving, I don't want it to end.

Chapter Ten

FLETCHER

We're still heated when we head outside, the extra jacket essentially useless...even as we slowly succumb to the cold, dry air on the way to my vehicle. White puffs of air freeze in front of us as we walk.

At my silver Ford F-250. I boost her into the passenger seat, leaning over to buckle her in before rounding the vehicle to turn it on and get the hot air blasting. Then, I scrape the windshields. Once back inside and driving, I follow Drew's directions to her vehicle, a white Corolla in serious need of snow chains to navigate this winter wonderland. She unlocks the trunk with her key fob, and I pull out her luggage, throwing it into the extended cab before we drive off.

The cab feels warm, and Christmas carols play softly in the background as we crunch along the icy roads. I maneuver the truck methodically to avoid slamming on my brakes. The wheels would lock in these conditions, sending us shuttling across the roadway like an out-of-control sled, thanks to the four-wheel drive. Snowflakes swirl and smash into the windshield, creating a disorienting, gravity-less effect like driving through a wind tunnel.

"Thankfully, the ski lodge is only a few miles from the hospital because I wouldn't want to drive back to Hollister tonight." I remember my earlier conversation with Mandy about still being able to use this place, and my stomach churns. I wonder if she intended it for a little getaway with Reggie? Ironic that Drew and I will end up using it instead.

My companion remains extra quiet, so I ask, "What's on your mind, sexy?"

"Just the strangeness of the whole day. I came here expecting to stay at the hospital with Reggie. And instead, I'm leaving with a white cowboy cardiologist who drives a massive truck and fits so many redneck stereotypes, I don't know what to think."

I laugh. "I'm not your average redneck, although I was raised with a country boy's mentality, I guess you could say. It must seem strange from a SoCal perspective, huh?"

"Let's just say if I were home right now, I'd probably be wearing a light sweater and enjoying the cool breeze coming off the Pacific. Not freezing my ass off in a mountain town."

"It does take a little getting used to," I reply, feeling my heart sink. Maybe Drew's right, after all. Perhaps we are from two worlds so very different we could never make things work. If that's the case, then why do I feel so damn drawn to her?

"Of course, if I had a sexy cowboy doctor like you to keep me warm, I think I'd be fine."

Her words make my chest swell with pride. "There are countless ways I'll keep you toasty and safe," I promise.

She smiles, warming my heart.

Clearing my throat, I grumble, "I hate to bring up a bad topic, but how'd you meet Reggie if you live in Los Angeles?"

"He's originally from LA but got a job a year ago in Ophir City."

"Did you ever consider moving here for him?" I inquire, hoping to plant a seed.

"Kind of." She nods. "But the relationship always felt like it was on shaky ground. I didn't want to make a life-changing move about something so uncertain."

"So, you noticed red flags, then?" I ask, leveling my gaze on her before looking back at the road.

"Yes, more than I wanted to admit."

"Don't beat yourself up. I'm guilty of the same thing with Mandy. I guess because I didn't think I deserved any better. I don't mean to get all mushy, but I didn't even know what better was until meeting you."

Beaming at me, Drew grabs my hand bringing it to her lips and kissing my fingertips one at a time. Never has such tenderness radiated from another person to me, and I can't get enough of it.

When we reach the lodge, I pull into the garage, helping her out and into the house. Fortunately, I had the maid in a few weeks ago, so the dust is cleared and the sheets and bedding freshly washed and changed. Inside, I turn on the lights before going for the thermostat. The lodge sits at a toe-curling fifty degrees, so I lean into the heat, turning it up nearly twenty degrees.

"Coats go here," I say, leaning forward to remove the two she wears, hanging them on the rack. "The bathroom's down that hallway as is the guest bedroom. I'll put your luggage in there. Feel free to take a shower and make yourself at home. Are you hungry?"

"Not especially, but thank you."

"Wine, egg nog, whisky, beer? What can I get you?"

"Do you have red?"

I nod. "Cabernet Sauvignon work?"

"That sounds lovely," she replies, her head craning to take in the place. Although only half the size of my cabin in Hollister, the ski lodge is a good two thousand square feet and contains three bedrooms, two bathrooms, and a half bath.

Rustic wooden couches and chairs invite guests to get cozy in front of the massive stone hearth.

"This place is beautiful, and I love how you've decorated it, Fletcher," she says, walking around slowly. She stops before a vintage photo from the 1960 Olympic Games in the neighboring Palisades Tahoe.

"Thank you. It'll be a lot cozier after I get a fire going." I beeline for the hearth, kneeling to make good on my word. While I work on kindling a fire and getting it well-established, Drew pokes around some more before heading down the hallway to the guest bedroom.

I call after her, "Feel free to borrow any of my clothes or robes if you need to." I hope she won't notice Mandy's clothes still in my closet. I've never wanted to purge them before, but with Drew here, I'm ready to start fresh, making space for her and a new future.

A half-hour later, Drew reappears wearing one of my big, fluffy black robes. She swims in the massive covering, making me laugh. But the thought of her wearing my clothes also makes my dick jump. Fuck, I'd love to call her mine permanently. I can't remember the last time I thought about any woman this way...not even Mandy.

This realization fills me with a strange mixture of joy and apprehension because nothing lasts forever. Nevertheless, forever sounds pretty damn good with Drew.

"Make yourself at home," I instruct, pointing out the tray of cookies on the table alongside two large pours of Cabernet Sauvignon. "If you'll excuse me, I'm going to take a quick shower. I'll be right back." It heartens me to see how she cuddles up on the couch, grabbing her glass of wine and smiling at me as if she belongs. She does, whether she knows it yet.

Fifteen minutes later, I've showered and jacked off to get my desires better under control. I don't know what it is about this woman, but she sets my body on fire, and I want her so badly it makes it tough to breathe in the same room with her. Despite what happened in the break room earlier, I don't want to pressure her into anything she's not ready for.

Padding along the carpet barefoot, I sit beside her on the couch, watching her appraise my blue and green flannel pants and white, tight-fitting, V-neck T-shirt. All my time working out pays off as desire curls and swirls in her mesmerizing amber and mahogany eyes. "Is there anything else I can get you?" I ask innocently.

The look she answers with could sear my clothes off...an outcome I'd happily explore with her.

"No, thank you," she says in that silky voice that makes my heart sputter and quiver. I'd be sure I had a problem if I weren't a cardiologist.

"Are you comfortable?"

"Yes," she says, smiling warmly. "This place is amazing, Fletcher. I love it. Do you come here to ski often?"

"That's a funny story," I say with a chuckle. "I'm a terrible skier. I'm pretty sure anything past the bunny slopes would land me in the hospital with a broken back or neck. Neither one sounds like much fun to me. But Mandy grew up skiing and was totally into it, so I bought the place to make her happy. I won't deny it's also come in handy over the past few years for times like this when I don't want to drive back to Hollister."

"I don't ski much, either. So, there's something we have in common. How far is Hollister from here?"

"About thirty minutes. But on a night like this, with terrible driving conditions, I expect it to take two to three times as long. Especially depending on what other bozos are doing on the road."

"By other bozos, I assume you're referring to me?"

I laugh, scooting closer to her as I grab my wine glass. "I

want to say 'no,' but I've never seen you drive. So, I guess I should hold off judgment until I get a better sense of your skills behind the wheel."

"Let's just say I've lived in Los Angeles County my whole life. So, snow is kind of a foreign concept to me. You know, best experienced on screen through Hallmark movies."

"Hallmark movies. Do you watch those?"

She nods enthusiastically. "Yes, I do. They're a great way to explore romance tropes."

"Alright, you told me a bit about the beats. Although we haven't finished discussing them as far as I can tell, what are tropes?"

"Tropes are familiar thematic ideas that reoccur in romances. Think of them as a shorthand way to let readers know what they'll get in your story. For example, enemies to lovers."

"Okay, so two people who aren't too keen on each other in the beginning but work it out?"

"Yes, or grumpy sunshine."

I raise a questioning eyebrow.

"You know, kind of like you and me. You showed up at Starbucks frowning with far too much on your mind. And you grumbled at me when our orders got confused, whereas I was the sunshiny one who stayed optimistic and smiling."

"So, grumpy sunshine would be one of our tropes?" I ask.

She nods. "So would opposites attract, fish-out-of-water, and forced proximity."

"Opposites attract, I get. But fish-out-of water?"

"Yes, because I'm the big city girl stuck in a small-town blizzard with a cowboy mountain man kind of guy." She moves a couple of inches closer to me as she says the words, and my heart jumps in my chest.

"Alright, and then what about forced proximity?"

"You know, the blizzard outside and us having to stay together in the same place even though we've only just met."

I clear my throat, wanting to kiss her so badly I can barely think straight. "That's why you're here with me. So that we can get to know each other better."

She nods. "Often, with forced proximity, you also have only one bed. But obviously, that doesn't happen much in real life since most people have guest bedrooms."

"So, you're telling me if I'd locked the guest bedroom before you got here and told you we had to share the same bed, you would be okay with that?"

She giggles. "Romance is all about fantasy, not reality."

"And how do these fit in with the beats you discussed earlier?"

"Well, forced proximity and adhesion go hand in hand." She draws even closer so that I can feel the warmth of her thigh next to my bent calf. Another trope you might throw in there is 'he falls first.'"

I swallow loudly. "He does. I mean, he has."

"Has he?"

"Yeah, and he's about to find some damn way to make the one-bed thing happen. Maybe remove the guest bedroom sheets and throw them in the snow. Would that do the trick?"

Drew moves even closer now so that our legs press together. "I'm far too smart a writer to fall for that."

I cover the distance between us, pulling her into my lap. "Well, what about that whole revenge sex scenario you mentioned earlier? Is that considered a trope, and if it is, could you tell me more about it, Drew?"

"If I didn't know better, I'd say you're trying to make me give away all the best-kept secrets of my trade," she teases in soft, low tones.

Wrapping my arms around her and drawing her urgently

against me so that she straddles me on the couch, I say seductively, "I want a lot more than your secrets, sexy."

Chapter Eleven

DREW

My hands palm Fletcher's handsome cheeks, and I savor the roughness of his afternoon stubble. It makes the sexiest scruffy sound against my fingernails as I lean in to taste his uber-soft, warm lips again.

"God, I love the way you taste," he growls deep in his chest, making my whole body rumble against his hard core.

"What do I taste like?" I ask, arching my eyebrows, inches away from his face.

"Like my future," he says without skipping a beat.

The answer is so smooth that I can't hold my tongue. "How many women have you said that to?"

He pauses, pulling back a couple of inches to look me in the eyes. His face is pensive for a moment before he replies sincerely, "You're the first woman I've ever said that to."

"I don't believe that for one minute," I reply, smacking his shoulder lightly.

"Why not?" he asks, his cheeks flushing.

"I mean, you're so handsome and accomplished. The women have to be falling all over themselves for you."

"I already told you," he says, wrapping his big hands

around my hips and pulling me tightly against his arousal. "I work sixty hours or more a week. That doesn't leave much time for socializing. And that's why I stayed with Mandy far longer than I should have. But I don't regret any of it now because it brought you to me."

I feel torn by his answer. If these words came from the guys I usually date, like Reggie, I would know them for what they are. The bullshit players spew. But if Fletcher's being sincere, as everything about his face and manners indicates, then I'm already in over my head, and I don't know what to think about it.

Me with a white redneck cowboy? The thought is preposterous, even as I straddle him, savoring his rock-hard cock against my inner thigh.

"But we're from such different worlds, Fletcher..."

"I don't care," he says, covering my lips with his.

I continue, "I mean, SoCal and Ophir City? It couldn't be more—"

"I like how talkative you are, sexy. But there are other things I'd like to do with your mouth right now," he says in grumbly tones, feathering his lips over mine.

"I just don't—"

His tongue delves into my mouth as he brings his hand up to my cheek, changing the angle of my head to deepen his penetration. Waves of desire lap through me from my scalp to my toes and everywhere in between, ebbing and flowing warmth and pleasure, and eroding all remaining self-control.

"You're a good kisser," I pant, pulling my lips away from his.

"Am I?" he asks with a lopsided grin.

"You didn't know that?" I inquire skeptically.

"Do you want to know the truth?"

His question piques my curiosity. "Of course."

"Mandy didn't like how I kissed or much else about me.

At least, after a while. Of course, she was into me in the beginning, but she was probably drunk much of the time now that I think about it. Sorry to bring up my ex again, but most of my experiences were with her."

"How many other women have you been with apart from Mandy?"

"A handful. I can give you the full rundown, if you like. But it might be a buzzkill. Probably not as many as you think, though. Like I said, medical school and the military kept me very busy over the years. So did residency and everything else I went through to get where I am today. But I'm clean, and I have condoms."

"I'm also clean. I had a regular checkup two weeks ago, and all was good. And before that, Reggie and I hadn't been together for three months. I'm on birth control, too. So, we don't have to use condoms unless you want to."

"I want you as close to me as possible, if I'm being honest. But if you want me to wrap it, I will, Drew."

I bite my lower lip, running my hands through his soft, silky hair. "Do you want to know how many men I've been with?"

He tenses his jaw until the muscle jumps. "I don't care about your past. All I care about is your present and your future...hopefully, our future."

"How can you talk like this when we still know so little about each other?" I ask, desire lodging in my throat.

"I don't know how to describe it, but I have this unshakable feeling about you. I've had it since the moment I met you, even though I was more or less a total dick at Starbucks."

"Well, you had to have *your* egg bites," I tease, letting out a soft sigh as his hands roam up and down my back, still covered by his robe.

His hands come around to the front, finding the tie and

undoing it. He pushes the fluffy fabric off my shoulders, revealing the sexy purple silk nightgown that I wear.

"I like you in purple silk and lace," he says breathlessly, bringing his hand up to tenderly caress the frilly edge of my top, his knuckles brushing over my nipples, drawing a ragged sigh from my lips. "Even more than I like my egg bites," he teases, letting his hand caress my neck and shoulders slowly and sensually before descending to my décolletage.

His thumb brushes over my collarbone, followed by his fingertips, as he says adoringly, "You have the most delicate neck and shoulders. So smooth and silky, and the color of your skin is fucking mesmerizing, Drew." He leans closer, tracing his tongue along the flesh at the nape of my neck until it sizzles. His lips are soft and supple, licking and teasing me as he explores every inch of my neck, shoulders, and collarbones, making me feel like the most cherished woman in the world.

"Fletcher," I whisper as he continues to cover me in open-mouthed kisses, descending lower with each round until he flirtatiously bites my nipple through the silk of my nightgown, wresting a dark moan from me.

"Is this meeting the requirements of your revenge sex trope?" he asks against the silk before teasing me with his tongue and teeth. His hands come up, palming my breasts more desperately as his mouth alternates between tits until I'm ready to beg him to lower my nightgown and taste me.

As if reading my mind, his eyes meet mine, searing me as he raises a questioning eyebrow, pulling the spaghetti straps of my pajamas over my shoulders. My breath shudders in my chest as desire shivers through me, and he asks quietly, "Are you good with this?"

"Yes, Fletcher, so good with it. I need you, baby."

"Good because I need you, too, Drew. So fucking much." His eyes shine black now, his pupils fully dilated as he pulls my nightgown down over my shoulders, revealing both of my large, ample breasts.

"You're so fucking beautiful. It hurts to look at you," he says in a raw, earnest voice. No man has ever made me feel so cherished or adored.

He strokes and caresses my breasts, every place he touches, causing a cascade of sparks to flow through my body. My heart pounds against my ribs, and my breath comes in shaky pants now as his thumbs tease and play with my nipples until they form firm peaks. His mouth claims my left tit, causing my whole core to shake as his demanding mouth covers me, and his thirsty tongue swirls and stimulates my nipple.

"Goddamn, you taste amazing, sexy," he says quietly, showering my breasts with more attention, devoting himself to the work of savoring every inch of me. My breath increases until I pant like I've been running a marathon, letting out a high-pitched cry as the throbbing between my legs turns painful.

His hands stray lower now, caressing and squeezing every inch of my flesh as he finds my waist and then my generous hips. Shivers of desire follow his touch, and I love how big and strong his hands are as they drop over my ass, kneading my flesh.

"Please don't stop," I urge as his hands find the edge of my nightgown, scuttling up underneath it. His mouth continues to claim me passionately, his kisses sizzling me and his stubble rubbing my cheeks raw. I'm going to have a beard rash tomorrow, but I don't even care, entirely absorbed by how his sensual tongue strokes and teases me, letting me know what else is on his mind.

Fletcher's fingers find the waistband of my G-string, tracing its edges down to the lips of my pussy before pushing it to the side. "No more granny panties," he says with enthusiasm, admiring them for a long moment. His thumb strokes through my wet folds, still sensitive from the break room, and I gasp with anticipation.

He lets out a deep groan. "Are you always going to be this wet for me, sexy?"

"Yes, baby."

"Yeah?" he says, smiling as his fingers follow his thumb, drenching himself in my arousal. I wonder what number Mandy did on this gorgeous guy to make him question my unbound desire. "I want you so fucking bad," he confesses against the shell of my ear. "You have no damn idea."

"Oh, I do have an idea. Can't you tell?" I reply with another gasp.

His thumb penetrates my slick channel, and he smiles seductively. "Do you want me wrapped or raw?"

"Raw," I say on an exhale.

"Fuck, Drew," he pants.

My hands turn greedily towards his pants. "I'm going to need you out of these, baby."

He nods as I pull myself up on my knees giving him room to push down his boxer briefs and pajamas, freeing his massive, erect rod. My eyes round, taking him in greedily.

"Is it okay?" he asks, waggling his eyebrows.

"I think you know it's more than okay," I answer, steadying myself with my hand on his shoulder as I hover over him.

He grabs my waist, holding me in place even though every cell in my body longs to draw down over him, sucking him greedily into my pussy.

"Just for the record, you can call this revenge sex if you like. But for me, it has nothing to do with anyone else and everything to do with you and me."

I nod in agreement, my pussy throbbing and aching to feel the heat radiating from his body inside of me. "Strangers to lovers, then?"

"What?" he asks, his eyes dark with lust.

"The trope. If this isn't revenge sex, then we have to call it strangers to lovers."

"I'm fine with that," he replies, grabbing my hips and sliding me slowly down over him until I completely sheath him in my wet, slick pussy.

He closes his eyes, ecstasy written all over his face, as he grips the silk folds of my nightgown gathered around my hips before sliding me up the length of his rock-hard rod and then pulling me hungrily back down again.

"You're fucking perfection," he says, opening one eye and cocking his head to the side. "Like hot, liquid heaven."

His head lowers, returning to my tits and sucking me one at a time in and out of his mouth and between his teeth as his hands drive me over him with increasing speed, angling my hips so that the large tip of his rod drives into my G-spot over and over, showering ecstasy down around me.

I can't breathe. I can't think. All I can do is pant and whimper, moan and scream as he takes me at an increasingly punishing pace until I unravel around him, gripping his cock and milking it with a greedy need. "Fletcher!" I scream, coming so hard my whole body quivers and trembles over him.

Taking his cue, he slams into me, his breath hissing in his throat as he comes with a devastating thrust, pulsing his heat in tremulous waves. My fingernails dig into his muscular back as his iron-strong arms wrap around my waist, holding me so tightly against him that I feel like we're one being.

Chapter Twelve

FLETCHER

"How did that compare to your romance novels?" I ask after finally catching my breath.

She palms my cheeks, still straddling my lap, my thick rod buried deep inside her warm, buttery core. "That was amazing, Fletcher. Way better than any words on any page."

"I don't know if I believe you," I say, raising an eyebrow.

"And why wouldn't you believe me?" she asks, stroking the stubble on my cheeks as she stares adoringly at me. If I didn't know better, I could almost convince myself she loves me. Maybe it's wishful thinking, but it's what I find myself fixated on and unable to move past the more time I spend with her.

"Because I haven't read any of your books yet. So, I don't honestly know what I'm competing against."

"You're not competing against anything," she reassures me. "I just want you to be yourself."

"Well, this is pretty much me, Drew."

"Good," she says, biting her thumb.

"Why good?"

"Because I like you," she replies, her face growing serious

as she strokes my face and hair. "I like you far more than makes any logical sense, considering we've only just met."

"I feel like I've known you for much longer, though. How is that even possible, sexy?"

"I don't know," she replies, shaking her head and rubbing her thumbs over my cheeks and lips, staring hard at me as though she's trying to memorize everything about me. "But I sense it, too. And I've never felt this way about anybody before, Fletcher." Tears pool in her eyes, telling me how sincere her statement is. "I don't know what to make of it, though. Because we couldn't be more different...from more different backgrounds."

I tangle my fingers in her curly hair, stroking her silky locks. "I told you, sexy. We were made to complement each other. I'm shy, and you're outgoing. I'm country, and you're city. I'm a scientist, and you're a creative. I'm hard, and you're deliciously soft and feminine. Like yin and yang."

"But how could we begin to make it work?" she asks, shaking her head. "I mean, I'm a city girl from SoCal. And you're happy with your country life in Hollister. And after what happened with Reggie, I don't feel like rushing into another long-distance relationship, even though I want to try to figure this out."

I clear my throat, feeling an acute pain in my chest that I've never felt before. "I'm nothing like Reggie, Drew, and things would never go that way between us. I would never allow it because I'm not that kind of guy. But we don't have to figure out the logistics tonight. Instead, let's enjoy getting to know each other better. Like we've been doing all evening. I have to say I've loved every moment of my time with you."

She smiles softly, kissing me. "You're right, baby. I shouldn't get ahead of myself. I'm going to go clean up. I'll be right back."

"Can I get you more wine?" I ask as she crawls off me, leaving my cock wanting more.

"Yes, thank you."

After returning wearing only her silky nightgown, she sits down between my legs, and I wrap my arms possessively around her. "I want to know everything about you, Drew. What your childhood was like. What you enjoyed doing as a kid. What you dreamed of becoming. Who your first boyfriend was. Everything."

"Really? That'll take all night."

"I'm fine with that," I reply, stroking her hair gently. "You're going to find out that I'm meticulous when it comes to researching what I'm interested in, and now that's you, sexy."

"Alright." She giggles, snuggling back into me. "But you have to tell me everything, too."

I shrug. "There's not much to tell, and I can be kind of reticent about my past. I'm the first one to admit it. But I'll let you pry whatever you want to know out of me."

Drew dives into her past with a gusto, as I guessed she would. She describes her family and childhood with vivid poetry that brings their personalities and experiences to life for me. Her parents are still married, and she has three sisters, all fans of her romance novels. Growing up, she wanted to be a writer and carried a small notebook and pen with her everywhere, ready to document her thoughts and feelings.

In high school, she didn't date much or stay out late because she was too busy reading until three in the morning. She devoured the classics and celebrated black writers, developing her unique style over time. With a blush, she confesses, "This might surprise you because I've never been with a white man before. But I write mostly IR romances...you know, inter-racial about white men and black women."

"Really?" I exclaim, not sure how I feel about this revelation. "Please don't tell me you're only interested in me for research purposes."

She laughs, smacking my bicep lightly with her arm. "No, silly, of course not. Believe me, I've had other chances to be with white men if I wanted to. But with you, there's so much more. Like our souls recognize each other. I'm sorry to get all romantic and emotional, but it comes with my line of work."

I hold her tightly, shivers of pleasure shuttling through me at her confession. "Don't apologize for anything, and I'm glad you feel it, too. I would hate for something this powerful to be one-sided."

"I can't imagine anything being one-sided that involves you," she counters, chuckling.

"You'd be surprised," I say gravely. "But I'm tired of focusing on the past. I want to focus on the present...on us. So, now that we've established you're not with me solely because of my skin color, what do you think? Have I met your expectations based on your romance novels?"

"You keep asking me that, Fletcher. But my books are all about fantasy...not reality."

"I'd like to bring those fantasies to life for you, if you'd let me?" I ask, kissing her neck gently until her pulse heightens and her eyes shut, pleasure written on her lips.

"And how do you propose to do that, baby?" she whispers, her voice tremulous.

I grab my cell phone from the coffee table next to the couch. "I'll read one of your sex scenes, and then we'll reenact it. What do you think?"

"Now, there's an idea," she says darkly with a laugh.

"You've done this before?" I ask, not sure I want the answer.

She replies firmly, "No man's ever been interested in reading what I write. You'll be the first, Fletcher."

"And the last, if I have my way," I growl deep in my chest.

"Are you country boys all this sure about what you want?" Drew asks, shifting to look over her shoulder at me.

"I can only speak for myself, sexy. But yeah, for once in my fucking life, I know exactly what I want, and I'm old enough and wise enough to realize I'd be an idiot to squander this opportunity."

She smiles sadly.

Before she opens her mouth, I add, "It's okay if you're not sold on us yet. I'm a patient man. I don't want you to feel pressured in any way."

"Thank you," she says, pressing her lips tightly together. "Now, back to that reenacting one of my sex scenes idea. I like it. In fact, I think it's a wickedly brilliant idea."

"Good," I smile, opening my phone. "Do you have a request?"

She shakes her head. "Surprise me."

Chapter Thirteen

FLETCHER

"Okay, then," I say, clearing my throat and going to Amazon, where I look up her pen name. The first book that comes up is called *Her Fated Mate*, which sounds like what I want to be, so I order it. Opening the novel while she melts into my arms, I flip through it until I encounter a promising love scene.

The Alpha hovered over her, his musky scent filling her nostrils as he wrapped his hands around her hips, drawing her ass up toward him at the perfect angle for penetration. With a confident motion, he buried himself in her sweet pussy, filling her completely and letting out a feral moan.

Pounding into her over and over again, the knot swelling at the base of his cock pulsed and grew as he reached his climax thrusting completely inside her with one aggressive stroke. She screamed out a mixture of pleasure and pain as the move locked his throbbing knot inside her hot, tight channel, imprisoning him in her slick paradise.

Extended fully within her, his cock painted the walls of pussy with his hot release, filling her with sheer ecstasy as he bred her into pleasurable oblivion. They lay knotted together for more than a half hour as cum continued to fill her, ensuring the Omega's heat would bear far more than the cementing of their shifter bond...

I grimace, setting my phone down and rubbing my hand over my face. I let out a long sigh, feeling wholly defeated before I even start.

"Is something wrong, baby?" Drew asks, knitting her brows.

"Yeah, something's wrong," I say, shaking my head. "What you describe in your book isn't even physically possible. And that's the physician in me speaking."

"Not even possible? Really?"

"If this is what you're after...well, I'm sorry, Drew. I can't do that for you, and no other normally functioning man can, either. Our dicks don't work that way."

"Wait, which book did you read?"

I flip to the table of contents and back to the cover. "*Her Fated Mate*."

The words barely leave my mouth before she bursts into giggles.

My heart drops into my stomach, and I cross my arms, frowning. "What are you laughing at?" I grumble, feeling more peeved by the minute.

She shakes her head, wiping tears from her eyes, unable to speak as she chuckles more. I know she's not laughing at me, but it still annoys me because there's nothing I want more in this world than to please her.

Finally, she manages, "Baby, you were reading one of my paranormal romance books. I wrote those at the beginning of my career. Gosh, I'd almost forgotten about them. I mean, that has to be at least twenty books ago."

"So?" I ask gruffly.

"Paranormal books like that about werewolves sometimes have the knotting kink in them."

"Knotting what?" I ask, shaking my head.

"A knotting kink. It's based on the real-life biology of canid species. Male canines have a bulbous gland at the bottom of their shaft that swells during copulation. It seals the male to the female, ensuring no semen leaks out while mating and improving the chances of impregnation. Some women get off on this kink in werewolf and shifter books because it represents the ultimate connection, and it also goes with the breeding kink and all of that." She's still laughing.

I run my hand through my hair. "I guess that makes sense. But it's not something I'm going to be able to do for you."

Drew turns in my arms, kissing me. "I'm not even into the knotting kink, baby. That was me dabbling in one of the many romance genres out there until I found my sweet spot."

"And what's your sweet spot?" I ask, squeezing her against me.

"Contemporary interracial urban romances."

"So, no dick knotting?" I laugh, starting to find the humor in the whole thing.

"No dick knotting... Hey, I have an idea. Instead of reenacting one of my love scenes, how about you provide me with some new material?"

"Is that a challenge?" I growl, feeling my cock come back to life.

"It is."

"In that case, you're coming with me," I declare, gathering her in my arms and lifting her as I stand up.

She covers her mouth with her hand, exclaiming, "I'm too heavy for you to carry like this?"

"The fuck, you're too heavy for me. I'm not even breaking a sweat," I counter, sauntering down the hallway to my bedroom. "It's time to explore the forced proximity and only one-bed tropes further, sexy. But first, it starts with you on your hands and knees on my bed."

I toss her gently onto the bed, and she laughs, staring up at me. "On my hands and knees?"

"That's right," I say, breathlessly.

"Did my fated mate saga inspire your sudden interest in doggy style?"

"I have more than that in mind," I promise in rich, low tones.

The gorgeous writer complies obediently, looking over her shoulder as I come behind her, sliding the slinky silk of her nightgown up over her round, smooth ass. "These have to go," I order darkly, sliding my hand under her G string and running my knuckles sensually over her ass.

"Ohh," she says with an appreciative groan as I bring my large hands up, removing the frilly strip. She lifts one knee at a time, helping herself out of them. Spreading her legs, my rough, large hands caress her round, beautiful ass, drawing little whimpers and sighs from her.

Goose bumps trail the places I touch, and I ask in a pant, "Are you cold, sexy?"

"No, just turned on," she says as I spread her ass cheeks, leaning in to eat out her pussy from behind. She stifles a high-pitched scream as my tongue slides through her delicious wet folds, enjoying my first taste of her apart from my fingers earlier.

"Damn, sexy, you taste fucking amazing. I could get addicted to you if I'm not careful."

"Maybe I want you to," she says, whimpering as I add my fingers to the mix, circling her arousal-slick clit as I tease her with my tongue from behind. My tongue laps at her greedily as my fingers spread her beautiful pussy folds, admiring the glistening arousal covering them.

I fuck her with my tongue, drawing in and out of her again and again and alternating sucking on her hard, engorged pearl. I suck and devour her deliciously silky pussy lips as her honey grows thinner and more slippery, begging for my thick cock.

Naughty wet sounds accompany my movements as I moan against her pussy, making her tremble. I don't stop until she's a drenched, hot mess, honey dripping to her knees and slick in all the right places, begging for me to fill her.

"How do you want me?" I ask, my voice ragged with desire.

"Facing me, baby. I want to look at you when we make love."

Make love. Her words put an unexpected warmth in my chest. I don't think Mandy ever talked about fucking me like that.

Drew's words awaken something in me that's been missing, and I didn't even know it. As much as I want to blow this woman's mind, I want to make love to her far more. I want to connect with her on every level, claiming her altogether as mine.

Swiping my hand over my drenched face, I flip her over onto her back, gazing lovingly at her breathtaking face. My fingers stroke her cheek, and I whisper, "I don't know what you're doing to me, sexy, but I fucking love everything about every moment we spend together."

"I do, too," she says, her large eyes pooling and generous lips trembling.

"I don't just want your body, Drew. I want your heart and your soul. I want everything about you..." I catch myself before adding "forever."

I bring her knees up so that I can slide easily into her warm, wet pussy, trembling at the feel of her humidity wrapped around me. Sex is so much more than getting off with her. It feels like connection and love. And it feels wonderfully like home, though I can't explain why.

Stroking her face with my fingers, I stare deeply into her

eyes, finding an intimacy and affection I've never felt with another human being. "What the fuck am I going to do with you?" I ask softly, my voice warm with emotion as I slide in and out of her, savoring every sensation of her silky body.

"Love me," she whispers.

"Done," I reply, trembling as she wraps her arms around me, her fingertips igniting trails of fire as they dance over my naked chest and back muscles, caressing and kneading the muscles until they dissolve into desire. Our lips meet, our tongues mating until we both pull away breathlessly, gasping for air.

"Fuck, you're the best thing that's ever happened to me," I say, crushing my mouth over hers again, climbing dizzying heights as I feel her pussy greedily clamping down around me, sucking me in and quivering and fluttering. I change my angle, driving deeper into her wet invitation and enjoying the primal sound of our flesh slapping together. She wraps herself around me, her fingernails digging into my back as she screams my name, melting around me in blissful surrender.

I pound into her until I explode, clasping her tightly against my hot chest and moaning her name like some kind of incantation. I would give anything to keep this woman who I haven't even known for a full twenty-four hours.

Chapter Fourteen

DREW

"You need to get the fuck out of here." Fletcher's angry voice awakens me, even though I can tell he's trying to speak in hushed tones.

"Whatever. It's not like you have anything going on. I told you nicely, I want to use the lodge one more time."

"No, Mandy. Leave and take Reggie with you. And give me your set of keys before you go."

"Hey, don't talk to my girl like that," I hear my ex's familiar, annoying voice. He stumbles drunkenly over his words, too.

"I don't want any trouble from either of you. But this is my property, and I'll call the sheriff's department if I have to."

"Calling your big brother on little old me? That's just like you, Fletch. You always were a coward."

The female voice slurs and sounds unsteady. But I don't care if she's drunk or his ex. Nobody's going to talk to Fletcher that way. Grabbing his fluffy black robe and pulling it on, I head towards the sound of the voices, storming into the living room.

A skinny, impeccably dressed blonde stands arm in arm

with Reggie at the front door. Both are red-faced and inebriated, and anger flashes across Fletcher's face as he realizes they've woken me up.

"Drew, what the fuck are you doing here?" Reggie asks, raising his eyebrows and shaking his head in disbelief as he pulls his arm away from Mandy.

"Well, I came here to take care of your sorry ass only to find out what I knew deep down inside all along...you lied about everything," I say, anger raising the intensity of my voice as I draw closer to him, pointing my finger aggressively in his chest. "I ended up in Mr. Anton Horowitz's room, who just so happens to be a patient of Dr. Knight. And I'm sure you know Dr. Knight, Mandy's ex, a man she likes to torture."

He grimaces, opening his mouth to speak but saying nothing.

"You know what's the one thing I can't figure out?" I ask. "Why, out of all the hospital rooms you could have entered and made the call from, did you choose four thirty-five in the cardiology department? You had to know Mr. Horowitz was Dr. Knight's patient."

He shrugs. "I guess I wanted to check out the competition... But how'd you end up here? Did you fuck him, Drew?" Reggie asks.

"That's none of your—" My voice stops in my throat as Fletcher steps forward, his face rigid with anger.

"If you ever talk about her like that again, we're going to have trouble."

"You want trouble? You fucking redneck bastard?"

Fletcher looks at me, his eyes narrowing. "Sorry about this." Without hesitation, he wheels around, punching Reggie so hard my ex stumbles backward, holding his jaw and grimacing.

"You want to go, motherfucker? Because I'm ready," the

cowboy growls, stepping forward and inviting Reggie to fight back.

Mandy runs between the two men, screaming, "Don't fight over me!" She's pathetic in her intoxicated state but certainly no worse than Reggie. I feel sick, wondering what I ever saw in him.

Fletcher gives her a disgusted look, shaking his head. "This has shit to do with you, Mandy. We're through. It's over and done, and I want my goddamned keys. But Reggie and I have an ax to grind when it comes to Drew because he's treated her worse than shit, and I won't put up with it. My woman deserves respect, and he'll give it to her."

"Your woman?" Mandy gasps, looking back and forth between Fletcher and me.

"Yeah, my woman," the cowboy growls.

Reggie holds his jaw, rubbing it and staring long and hard at Fletcher. "C'mon, Mandy. Let's get the fuck out of here." The discrepancies between these men couldn't be more obvious. Reggie looks downright skinny and weak compared to the well-built cowboy, and his arrogant veneer melts into beta cowardice.

The rail-skinny blonde with too much makeup raises her eyebrows, her face irate. "Are you seriously going to let Fletcher talk to me like this?"

Reggie shrugs. "Mandy, you told me this place was free and available, but obviously, it isn't. I'm done. Let's go."

The blonde shoots a furious look at Fletcher before making her disgust evident as she eyes me, recognizing the doctor's robe.

Through clenched teeth, Fletcher replies, "That's one of your many chief talents, Mandy, making men done... completely fucking done with you."

She humphs, her face agitated. "You're driving, Reggie."

"Neither one of you is driving," Fletcher butts in begrudgingly. "I'm calling you an Uber. But you can park your sorry asses in the garage until it gets here. Grabbing his phone, he pulls up the app, searching for a few minutes until he finds someone willing to drive in this weather. "This is going to cost an arm and a leg."

Reggie grimaces, and Mandy spouts, "He's fully capable of driving. We don't need you calling anybody."

"Yeah, you do, so please keep your mouth shut," the cowboy says with a satisfied grin. "That's something I should have told you about five years sooner. But whatever. At least I won't have your drunk driving accident on my conscience. Now, give me those damn keys. Mandy." After he has them in hand, he turns to me. "Drew, baby, why don't you go back to bed? I'll be behind you shortly."

A half-hour later, the big, burly cowboy crawls into bed behind me, snuggling me in his arms. "You're cold, baby," I say with a shiver in my voice as he wraps his frigid, naked torso around me.

"And you're hot as fuck, sexy. Just the way I like you." He pulls the hair back from my neck, nuzzling into me. "Do you want to talk about what happened earlier with Reggie and Mandy?"

"No, baby," I say, snuggling back against his rigid body. "They're in our past now, and I don't want to waste more energy on either of them."

"But you came here for Reggie, and so much has happened. It has to be a lot to process."

His caring voice and understanding words touch my heart, and I pause for a moment, thinking through everything that's happened. After some quiet reflection, where I savor the feel of his flesh pressed against mine, I say, "I think I always knew deep down that Reggie was cheating on me. And maybe that's why I decided to come up here in the first place, unexpectedly and out of nowhere because I was tired of being played the fool. It was such a dissatisfying relationship, and he always made me feel unworthy. The worst part of it was I let him do this to me. Why did I do that, Fletcher?"

He holds me close, showering my neck and shoulder in tender kisses. "I've been asking myself the same thing about Mandy. There was no intimacy between us, no real affection. But I clung to her for years because it was the easiest thing to do, and a part of me believed I didn't deserve any better. Or at least I didn't know to expect any better...until I met you."

"I can see that from your point of view," I say, tangling my fingers with his. "After all, you grew up in a foster home. I don't know what it was like, but I'm guessing you didn't have many loving couples to look to for inspiration."

"Not really," Fletcher says quietly. "By the time I showed up, my foster dad, Wyatt, was already a widower. His wife, Ruby Jean, died of cancer. My older foster brothers spoke fondly about her, but she was always a memory to me. Nevertheless, Wyatt set an amazing example for me of what a man should be."

"Yes, he did," I say, snuggling into him. "But where does that leave me, Fletcher? I grew up with both parents in my home. I saw a couple together for years. Why would I settle for so much less for myself?"

"I don't know. But maybe seeing your parents made you extra loyal...willing to forgive and forget more than most to make things work over the long haul. With Reggie, it was a flaw that he took advantage of. But with a guy like me, that tendency would be a strength...the kind of strength that would help me be a better man."

"No matter what we talk about, you keep circling back to our compatibility...all the ways we complement each other."

"I'm sorry if I sound like a broken record, Drew. But when I want something...truly want it, nothing will change my mind. I realize this is not all about me, though, and I don't want to pressure you."

"No man has ever made me feel safer or more loved than you do, Fletcher. And that's all I want to focus on right now..."

"And how do you propose focusing on that?" he whispers against the shell of my ear.

"I want to feel you inside me again, baby," I invite.

He grumbles against my back, "Good, because that's right where I want to be." His big hands push the silk of my gown up, seizing my hips and angling my ass up towards him.

His thick cock rests against my hip, poking me with its firmness. "You're already hard, baby?" I ask breathlessly.

"Let's just say it's more or less a constant state in your presence. Why do you think I call you 'sexy'?" He brings his hand between my legs, sliding his fingers and thumb through my wet folds. "And you're drenched for me again."

"Always, baby. My pussy's greedy for that big, juicy cock of yours."

He groans pleasurably at my words. His thumb circles my clit slowly and sensually. "This may go without saying, but it's all yours, Drew. Every fucking inch of it for as long as you want it."

"Yeah?" I ask, urgency coloring my voice as I tip my ass up some more, a breath away from begging him to take me.

Fletcher slides his erect cock through my folds enticingly, mixing the pre-cum dripping from his cock with my honey. Slowly and with great care, he slides into me, inch by inch, as he kisses the shell of my ear and neck, showering me in tender caresses. "What beat is this, Drew?"

I push back into him, taking him as deeply as I can as he tangles his hands in my hair, pulling me possessively towards him and lightly biting my shoulder. He squeezes my neck with his right hand, just enough to send a rippling thrill through me.

There's only one beat on my mind, but should I say it? His other arm wraps around my waist so that our bodies sensually snake together as he continues thrusting into me, leading me towards the edge of another orgasm.

I gasp, "Some writers would call this the happily ever after."

His cock is the perfect length to hit my G-spot relentlessly. "I like that," he says, expertly mastering my clit with his thumb. I shut my eyes, savoring every moment and focusing hard not to come yet.

Never in my life have I willfully held myself back. But it's the natural response to a man who will do anything to please me, taking his time and worshipping the hell out of my body until I finish, sated and glowing.

His hands find my breasts, stroking my nipples into stiff peaks, and his mouth dances over my flesh, feasting on me until I drive my hips back into him, screaming, "Fletcher!" I come so hard, I drench him, and he growls deep in his throat.

"Yes, sexy," he pants, seizing my hips and squeezing hard, taking me at a punishing pace until hot waves of cum fill me, and his hard body shudders behind me. Screaming my name, his body tenses as wave after wave of lust grips him until he collapses around me.

We lie in silence, tangled together as our breathing slows. Burying his head in the crook of my neck, he says softly, "Drew, we have a problem."

"What is it, baby?"

"I can't let you go. I'm sorry. I can't help myself, but I fucking love everything about you, including the way you feel in my arms like this."

"I love everything about you, too," I reply, feeling my heart thump wildly against my ribcage.

Chapter Fifteen

DREW

"Merry Christmas," I hear Fletcher's voice next to my ear. "I hate to wake you, sexy, but the world seems hellbent on bothering us tonight. I just got called into the hospital. Mr. Horowitz isn't doing well."

I shake my head, trying to clear the drowsiness like cobwebs. "Mr. Horowitz? I'm coming with you."

"How did I know you were going to say that, sexy?" the cowboy grumbles.

I grab Fletcher's hand, squeezing it. "I'll dress quickly. I don't want to make you wait."

The ride to the hospital is quiet between the exhaustion we both feel and my concern over Mr. Horowitz. I wonder if Fletcher gets nervous about seeing patients who aren't well. What must it feel like to be a doctor, exercising the responsibility of life or death over another person? But I don't want to ask questions now or throw him off in any way.

After parking, he grabs my arm, leading me quietly inside, his brows knitted and his face rigid. "You'll have to stay in the cardiology waiting room. But I'll keep you posted on everything."

"Can a nurse help me with contacting his family? He has a daughter that he's estranged from. I don't think she even knows he's at the hospital."

Fletcher searches my face, holding me tightly in his arms as the elevator climbs to the fourth floor and cardiology. "Molly was on shift earlier. I think it'll be Cliff next. I'll make introductions so you can see what's possible. Okay?"

"Thank you, baby. You don't know how much this means to me." The elevator door chimes open, and we step out.

"Will you say a quick prayer with me, Drew? Mandy always refused to do that for me because she doesn't believe in a higher power. But I hope you do, and I know I'm convinced of His existence. I could use His guidance and wisdom now."

"Yes, I believe, and I pray daily," I say, grabbing his hands. We bow our heads for a moment while I speak into the silence. Then, we head for the double doors, where he scans a pass, and we enter his department.

Striding faster now, the doctor quickly introduces me to Cliff. "She has a verbal from Mr. Horowitz to know about his medical and personal information, so please help her out," he calls over his shoulder, disappearing down the hallway.

Twenty minutes later, I sit in the cardiology waiting room, my cell phone pressed against my ear. It rings one, two, three times before a tired voice answers. "Hello?"

"Hello, I'm sorry to bother you at this early hour," I say. "But I need to speak with Georgia Horowitz, please."

"Speaking. What's going on? I see you're calling from Ophir City Hospital."

"Your father, Anton Horowitz, is a patient with the hospital, and he wanted me to call to let you know."

"He is? Oh my gosh, what's wrong?" she asks, a tremble in her voice.

"I can't give you those details over the phone, but I know it would mean a lot if you could come see him for Christmas."

"Yes, I can do that."

"I hate to worry you, but the sooner you get here, the better. Is this the best number to communicate updates to you?"

"Yes, this is my cell phone. I need to get dressed, and then I'll head your way. Dad is so poor at keeping me informed about what's going on with him healthwise, and I know he's still mad at me for pushing for Mom to go into a memory care facility towards the end of her life. So, I appreciate you letting me know."

"Of course. Please drive carefully and keep me posted on when you get here."

Nearly three hours later, I sit in the waiting room with a middle-aged woman with short, curly white and red hair. She's got large, curious eyes like her father, but lacks his bravado or authoritative way of speaking.

Licking her lips, she says, "Dad never forgave me for intervening when Mom was in the later stages of dementia. She made him promise that he'd never put her in a nursing home. But towards the end, she was a flight risk and a fall risk, which was tough. We tried having in-home nurses, everything. But eventually, Mom had to go into a nursing home. And that's when Dad stopped talking to me."

I lean forward, hugging her. "That had to be so hard."

"It was," she says, wiping her hands over her face. "That's why I can't thank you enough for calling and letting me know what's happening. So, how did you first meet my dad?"

"It's a long and strange story," I say, shaking my head. "How much time do you have?"

"All the time in the world, considering it's only six forty-five," she says, eyeing her watch.

"Shall we head down to the cafeteria to get a hot drink or something and talk?"

"We can, but I want to be here as soon as Dr. Knight has something to tell us."

"I promise, my cell phone's at the top of his list," I reply with a wink. We head downstairs together to share hot cocoas and sit by the giant Christmas tree with sparkling lights that Fletcher and I danced by yesterday evening.

I fill her in on every part of the evening related to her dad until my cell phone rings. I answer it, and Fletcher's deep voice greets me. "Drew, Mr. Horowitz is stabilized, and he's asking to see you. Did you have any success reaching out to his daughter?"

"Yes, she's with me now."

"Good, because I think the stubborn old guy's finally seeing things for what they are, and he'd like to reconcile with her."

"Still four thirty-five?"

"No, he's in our intensive care wing now. One floor down, so three thirty-six. I'll meet you there."

Fletcher stands in front of Mr. Horowitz's new room, shaking hands with Georgia. She asks about her father's condition, and he promises to fill her in as soon as he has a verbal from her father regarding his medical information.

I feel strange knowing more about her father's condition than she currently does. However, once we enter Mr. Horowitz's room, he permits everyone in the room to discuss his condition. A male nurse sits near his bed, monitoring the musician's condition. His name badge reads Heath Hetherington.

Mr. Horowitz eyes me with a big grin, saying, "Sorry to ruin your night, Drew. How did your date with Dr. Knight go?"

I grab his cold hand, squeezing it gently. "Beautifully. Perfectly. You couldn't have been more right about the two of us. Thank you, Mr. Horowitz."

He nods, his face paler than before. "Good. Like I said, when you've lived this long, you know things. And who is this?" he asks, staring long and hard at his daughter.

"Dad, it's me," Georgia says, stepping forward to take his hand from mine as I step back, tears filling my eyes.

"Honey, it is you," he says, his eyes pooling with emotion. "What are you doing here?"

"I'm here to spend Christmas with my dad."

She takes a seat, and her father smiles. Looking over her head at me, he says, "Thank you, Drew. You were right about this, too. And thank you, Dr. Knight."

"Of course," Fletcher says as I nod, smiling warmly. The doctor grabs my hand, leading me out of the hospital room. "Are you always this good at bringing loved ones together during the holidays?"

"I try," I say, smiling as he wraps his arms around me. "But I feel kind of bad, Fletcher, because I have nothing for you for Christmas."

"You've already given me more than I could ever imagine having. You've healed my heart in ways I can't describe, Drew. Ways I didn't even know were possible. I can't thank you enough for sharing this holiday season with me, and I sincerely hope, with every ounce of my being, that this is the beginning of so much more." He leans into me, feathering his lips gently over mine.

"About that," I say softly, taking a deep, steadying breath. "We've learned so much about each other over the past day. But we have yet to discuss our current lives and the logistics behind trying to make something like this work."

"Can we save that for after Christmas, sexy? Right now, I want to focus on savoring every moment I can with you."

I nod, settling into this much easier proposition, even as I wonder what our future holds.

Chapter Sixteen

FLETCHER

I hold Drew tightly, nuzzling her neck and kissing her softly. We've spent a week together, and this is the day I've been dreading. The day she has to drive back to Southern California to attend a writer's conference where she's the keynote speaker.

I would love to attend it and hear her talk. The more she tells me about her career, the more intrigued I become. But I've got a full schedule that doesn't bend for anyone, even the woman I want to spend the rest of my life with.

"How the fuck do I begin to let you go?" I ask, not even trying to hide the rawness in my voice.

She pulls my arms more tightly around her, snuggling back into me. "I'm going to miss waking up next to you. But we'll have to get used to this side of our relationship, too. After all, we're both very hardworking individuals. And although I haven't talked much about it, I easily work sixty hours a week, too."

"Great, so we're both workaholics?" I grumble.

"We're both very ambitious, driven people, baby."

"But not at the expense of our relationship. We have to make that promise to each other."

My chin rests atop her head, and I feel her nod. "Fletcher, I don't want to leave you...ever."

"So, you finally get how I feel? What changed?" I ask, my heart expanding with relief, knowing I'm not alone in my need for her.

"This has been the best week of my entire life. No man has ever made me feel so loved and protected. You can't get enough of me, and I obviously can't get enough of you. And for the first time, I see how a lifetime together could work with another person. I feel like years could pass in the blink of an eye, wrapped up in your love and support...without drama or angst or any of that awful stuff that marked my past relationships. They were all terrible before you. Not just Reggie."

Her words invigorate my resolve to keep her. "Don't leave then," I say firmly.

"I wish I could stay, but I have so much to work out back home. We have so much to figure out."

"And we will. Together. We'll make this work, sexy. I promise. I'll visit you whenever possible, and you can head my way when it makes sense. We live in the same damn state, after all. We can make this happen."

She nods. "Yes, we're only seven hours apart by car and less than two by plane."

"That's right, sexy."

She shrugs. "That said, long-distance relationships can be a challenge. They can be difficult. It's so easy to grow apart when leading separate lives."

"We can't let that happen."

"But how do we stop the inevitable?" Her voice trails off sadly.

"By not letting it become inevitable," I reply, half tempted to ask her to marry me but knowing it's not the right time. I've already pressured her more than I should because I can't help myself when it comes to her.

"I'm so afraid to lose you, Fletcher. And I don't want things to ever get bad between us. You know, like so many long-distance relationships end."

"We won't let that happen. We can't."

Drew turns towards me, stroking my face. "Have you ever thought that maybe this is as good as it will get? That we should thank God for the time we've had together and not try to make it anything more than it is? Because by adding unrealistic expectations, we stand to ruin everything?"

I feel my heart stop and grip my chest, taking a deep breath. "Okay, no, I haven't thought that for one moment, and I don't want to start thinking about it now. You sound unsure of us, Drew? Almost like you're resigned to a certain outcome no matter what. But what if we don't want it to go that way? There have to be other options, right?"

She smiles sadly, taking in my face meticulously, as if trying to remember how I look. It fills me with apprehension, casting a pall of finality over the moment. "I hope so, baby. I hope so with all my heart."

I stroke her cheek as my mind races. "I don't know what you're thinking right now, Drew. But I want to be with you, and I'll do whatever it takes to make that happen. Whether that means you moving here or me relocating to SoCal. In the meantime, I'm going to prove to you how committed I am to making this work until you see things the way I do."

"Relocate to SoCal? But all your family's here, and you have a thriving career in Ophir City."

I knit my brows together. "None of that means a thing without you, sexy. Don't you get it? I need you with me today...tomorrow...for as many tomorrows as we can imagine having together."

"It's what I want, too, Fletcher. We'll stay in touch and

figure this out. I promise." But her face looks far sadder than it should, and I can't shake the feeling she's slipping through my fingers.

"Tell me what you need from me. Whatever it is to reassure you, I'm in this for the long haul."

"We'll take it one beat at a time like we've been doing, until everything happens the way it's supposed to."

She continues to talk resignedly as she packs her clothes and prepares to head to the hospital with me. After helping her dig out and putting new snow chains on her tires, I talk her through when and where she'll likely be able to remove them, handing her a wad of cash to pay for help.

"I wish I could come with you. I'd love to drive you back to your place. But the work of a cardiologist never ends."

"Neither does that of a romance writer," she replies, smiling sadly.

I pull her into my arms, kissing her hard and long. "You may not want to hear this, sexy, but I fucking love you. So, we need to make this work. Okay?" I rest my forehead on hers, and she nods, pressing her lips together as if she has more to say.

Instead, she replies, "I love you, too, Fletcher. And I always will."

Chapter Seventeen

DREW

I head south through a flood of tears, putting miles between Fletcher and me. It's the only logical thing to do, even though I love him so much I can't fathom what tomorrow will feel like without him. I remind myself that he's less than two hours away by plane, but the intensity of this past week makes any separation excruciating.

Still, I can't suspend my life and career because of an unexpected romance. I have responsibilities and life back home, and I have to have faith that everything will work. Just like Fletcher kept saying this morning. Having that faith feels tough, though, considering my past relationships. But Fletcher is different, and so are my feelings for him.

I turn up the satellite radio, blaring Christmas carols to lighten the mood in the cab of my car. Nevertheless, I continue sobbing and driving, my mind flooding with memories of our amazing week together.

These memories remain so recent I experience them with all five senses. I feel his soft, warm lips brushing over mine, teasing and tasting me. His hot muscles pressed against my soft curves, his hands tangled in my hair, his heart beating next to mine as we become one again and again, unable to satisfy the unquenchable thirst for each other.

At a stop light, I glance at my phone, seeing he's already texted me:

> I love you and miss you, sexy. Drive carefully and keep me posted on where you're at and when you make it safely home

A part of me wants to pull over and call him. But I've got to get a hold of myself. I'm a best-selling romance writer with a book becoming a movie. I've got to get my head screwed back on straight.

My phone screen lights up, and I answer, hearing my personal assistant's voice. "Long time no talk, Drew. I thought you fell off the face of the Earth or something."

"Sorry, Cassidy. Things have just been insanely busy with the holidays and all."

"How was your mini vacation with Reggie? How bad are his injuries?"

I shake my head at her question. She is so behind on everything that's happened. *Where to start?*

I take a deep breath. "Before we talk personal matters, fill me in on what's going on. How are the Facebook Ads performing? How's the Street Team doing with building momentum around the new release?"

"Oh, you're ready to dive right in? Okay, well, you're getting a cost per click of seventeen cents with the Facebook Ads, which is about as good as you're going to get. And your Amazon sales are through the roof."

I clear my throat, scolding myself for letting my mind wander to thoughts of Fletcher's gorgeous muscular physique and the slow lovemaking we indulged in this morning before parting...as if he wanted to find a way to keep us together forever.

"What do you mean by 'through the roof?'"

"Let's see here. You're currently at one hundred thousand page reads for the new book, and reviews look good across the board. Bookstagram is on fire with promos from your Street Team and influencers. This is shaping up to be one of the best releases you've ever had..."

"And despite the fact I took an extended vacation, refusing to focus on business? How bizarre. It's almost like the universe is rewarding me for not micromanaging things."

"Yes, apparently focusing on Reggie has had a beneficial effect on your career and book sales. Who'd have guessed that?"

"I wasn't with Reggie," I finally say in deep tones.

"Not with Reggie?"

"That's right. I met somebody new, and I don't even know how to begin describing him...except he's perfect."

"Well, you'll have to try because I'm on pins and needles over here. And you also need to fill me in on what happened with Reggie...or more like what didn't."

"Reggie cheated on me, and I caught him red-handed."

"Oh, honey, I'm so sorry to hear that." Although Cassidy goes through the motions verbally, I can tell by the tone of her voice that none of this surprises her.

"Yeah, but then the strangest thing happened. I got to know the ex-boyfriend of the woman with Reggie now, and all I can say is sparks flew."

"What? How did that happen?"

"It's a long story..."

"And you have a long drive, so out with it," Cassidy orders, sounding more like my boss than my employee.

"So, Reggie lied about the whole ski injury thing. Instead, he was planning on a ski vacation with a coworker named Mandy. Mandy is the recent ex of a doctor at the hospital named Dr. Fletcher Knight, and I ended up meeting him by accident after visiting the hospital room where Reggie told me he was staying. It turned out to be somebody else's room. The cutest little old guy in the world, Mr. Horowitz, and after I got to know him, I met his physician, Fletcher. And he's the most amazing man I've ever met in my entire life."

"Really? Tell me more about this Dr. Fletcher guy."

"Well, he's a former Army cardiologist working full-time at Ophir City Hospital. He's highly esteemed in his field. I mean, you can look him up online and see..."

"Already doing that. God, he's gorgeous!"

"He is, isn't he?"

"And?"

I take a deep breath, so overwhelmed by everything I have to tell her that I struggle to know where to continue. "Well, we fell for each other, and leaving him is one of the most painful things I've ever done..."

"But it's only for a little while, right?"

"I hope so."

"If what he said is true, I can't imagine you'll be waiting long."

I sigh. "I hope you're right. But if past relationships have taught me anything, words are a dime a dozen, and actions are everything. So, we'll have to wait and see what the doctor's next moves are."

"Honey, you should marry this guy. He looks and sounds perfect for you."

"Last time I checked, guys are supposed to do the asking when it comes to marriage," I remind.

"Maybe it's time to change that," Cassidy replies firmly. "Remember that romance you wrote for leap year? You had the girl propose in that one, and it remains one of your most consistent best-sellers."

"I know. I know. But for once in my life, I don't want to feel like I'm doing all the chasing and trying to make things work. If he really wants me, then he needs to pursue me. After all, I'm not hard to find."

"Oh, it sounds like he's definitely going to come looking for you."

"I hope so, Cassidy, because I'm head over heels for the guy..."

My screen lights up with a new notification from Fletcher. I pull it up, reading:

I fucking miss you, Drew

I sigh sharply.

"What?" Cassidy asks.

"Fletcher keeps texting that he loves and misses me."

"He sounds amazing, Drew. You've got this guy in the bag."

"We'll see," I say, pulling over to text him back.

I love and miss you too baby and I need to see you again

You don't have to ask twice. The first chance I get I'm there to lick that delectable pussy of yours and make you all mine again and again. You've fucking broken me, sexy, all I can think about is u

Chapter Eighteen

FLETCHER

A month has passed since meeting Drew, and we've texted, called, and commuted to be together every chance we get. It's not nearly enough, though. I've met her family, and they love me. And my family adores her. But loving her has made me incredibly impatient. I know what I want with her, and I don't see why we have to wait. Drew agrees with me. I sense it when we're together, but she's more worried about looking sensible.

All I know is I don't give a damn what anybody else thinks, and I won't rest until she's mine. What we have is far too special to fuck around with. Besides, a wedding can easily take a year or more to plan, an eternity to be away from my sexy girl.

Which brings me to my current situation... Slinking into The Human Being Cafe to participate in something I never would have considered before meeting Drew—a romance book club. Fuck me.

Fortunately, I can't be too intimidated because I know every woman seated around the table in the back of the cafe. There's my sister-in-law Roxy with her long black braids. She's a Wa-She-Shu woman married to my foster brother, Hawk, a Shoshone-Bannock helicopter pilot.

Her bestie, Shelby, a Paiute woman who used to work at the local diner, sits next to her. Rounding out the table are The Human Being's redheaded owner, Delilah, and two more of my sisters-in-law, Jess, a blonde true crime reporter, and Alex, a classical cellist with a mane of black curls and crystal blue eyes.

I'm also surprised to see Effie with her black hair in a pixie cut. The kindergarten teacher has kind lavender eyes, an upturned nose, and bright cheeks. She's always got a smile on her face and works at Hollister Elementary. The paragon of wholesomeness, she couldn't be a more unlikely associate of my foster brother, Rock, who owns the only tattoo parlor in town, Wicked Skin. But they've been seen enough together in recent months to get the wheels of the small-town rumor mill turning. And he brought her to Christmas at the ranch, which tells me there's more to their story than he's disclosed.

None of the romance reader club members look surprised when I saunter in their direction, making my way around the table to hug everyone. They don't even blink when I sit down. But when six o'clock rolls around, ushering in the beginning of their meeting, all eyes focus on me.

"I'm sorry to put a cramp in your style. But I'm here for help from you self-professed romance readers."

"Okay," Roxy says, raising her eyebrows and whipping her black braids around as she bobbles her head between me and the rest of the women seated at the table.

"How do I put this?" I think out loud, looking at the ceiling for a moment. I really am a shy guy by nature, but I also pursue what I want with steely determination. And right now, I need the best advice I can get. "You've all met Drew, and you know how amazing she is. And you also know she's a famous romance writer, which is why I need advice on how to clinch the deal with her."

"Thank God for Drew," Jess exclaims. "What a breath of fresh air after that Mandy woman."

"Hell, yes," Delilah chimes in, making her Bohemian dress and costume jewelry rustle as she shifts towards me. Effie nods, flashing her usual contagious smile.

"But what do you mean by 'clinch the deal?'" Alex asks, blinking at me.

"Like make her mine forever," I say breathlessly. "Because I'm totally, madly in love with her. But she thinks we're rushing, and I'm fucking miserable in a long-distance relationship. I need her by my side all the time."

"But you've only recently gotten together, right?" Shelby pipes in, fixing her cinnamon-colored eyes at me.

"Yes, we met a month ago," I confirm.

"That's fast," Effie says.

Jess chimes in, "When you've met the right person, you just know. I mean, look at Logan and me. We'd both sworn off marriage and long-term relationships forever. But we ended up married within six weeks of meeting."

Alex nods, "And while Maksim and I spent nine months planning a big wedding, we moved in together within a week of meeting. We couldn't do it any other way because he's no good without me. And I hate being without him."

"He's a downright fucking recluse without you," I confirm, nodding my head. "Barely functioning in society."

"I know," Alex says, her cheeks flushing.

Shelby smiles. "I guess I can't really talk, either. I mean, Farzad and I had known each other from a distance for nine months, but once we got together... Well, we got married the next day."

"See, that's what I'm talking about. But Drew thinks this is all crazy talk, which I find insane, considering she's a romance author. And I know in her heart of hearts she wants to be with me right now, too. So, I've come to the conclusion I'm doing something wrong, and I need your help."

"Hmm..." Roxy says, shaking her head. "What if she really just needs more time?"

"That could be. But we're both so career-focused. We each easily work sixty hours a week, which makes me afraid we'll grow apart if I don't make it clear how committed I am to her. The last thing I want is for her to slip through my fingers. And I also want desperately to care for her, provide for her, and protect her."

"Why not just date and see where it goes? Without too much pressure?" Jess asks, but I can tell by the look on her face she's playing devil's advocate. She does that a lot, thanks to her journalistic training.

"Because there's no one else on this planet for me. I'm not opposed to a long engagement or whatever she needs, but I don't want to live apart anymore. I need to come home to her at night and wake up to her in the morning. I've waited thirty-four years to find her."

Shelby smiles. "Farzad said something similar to me when he proposed. When you know, you just know."

"That's right." I pull out my notes as I speak to make sure I get everything right. "Now, the last time Drew and I discussed our relationship and where it was headed, she said that if we were doing things by the beats in a romance, we'd be on the happily ever after. Or, at a bare minimum, the hot sex scene. Sorry if that's TMI. But I figure you ladies can handle it with the kind of shit you read. So, what am I missing?"

"The hot sex scene to the happily ever after?" Roxy says, twisting her mouth. For a second, I think she's grossed out, but then I realize she's deep in thought.

Jess adds a caveat. "Just for the record, none of us are actual romance writers, but hmm...I would feel a little dissatisfied as a reader to jump straight from the hot sex scene to the happily ever after. Don't you think?" she asks, looking around the table.

Alex nods. "Yeah, it would be missing a lot. Like, you know, the third act breakup and all of the angst."

I frown deeply. "I'd like to avoid that, if at all possible." My heart aches acutely, seconding my statement.

"Of course," Delilah says in her most comforting voice. "And luckily, not all romances do the third act breakup anymore. But if you're looking for missing beats...well, there should definitely be a grand gesture of some sort."

"A grand gesture?" I ask, sitting up straighter. "Now, that sounds more like what I'm after. Tell me what a grand gesture looks like."

The women dive into countless examples of dramatic displays of affection as I take notes. The grand gestures differ wildly, but they all share the same basic theme, making yourself completely and utterly vulnerable to the person you love. The thought of this scares the shit out of me, but losing Drew scares me even more. So, I keep jotting down ideas even when my heart pounds in my chest and my head spins.

Once they give me plenty to mull over, they ask me questions about Drew and what her family and life is like in SoCal. I love fielding their inquiries, and they squeal and cheer when I get a text from her telling me how much she loves and misses me.

"Fuck, I love this woman," I tell them with a big smile.

"We couldn't be happier for you," Jess says with a contagious grin. "We've only ever wanted happiness for you. You deserve it more than anyone."

"Well, Drew makes me happier than I've ever been. But it also means I feel completely miserable without her. Yes, I'm rushing things, but I'm tired of living without her. Even if it means relocating to SoCal. I'm down for whatever, as long as we're building a life together."

Alex chimes in, "I certainly hope Drew will consider moving here. I know it's a big jump from LA. But coming from San Francisco, I have to say I adore this place."

"Me, too," Jess chimes in. She and Alex are besties, and she's also from San Francisco.

Delilah adds in, "We'd love to have *the* Drew Devereaux living in our town, although ultimately, we want you to be happy."

"I'll be happy wherever Drew is," I say emphatically.

They nod, asking more questions about Drew and helping me hone in on the types of things that she likes and what might impress her.

"All I know is whatever I do needs to be big and unforgettable. The kind of thing she'll remember fondly until the day she dies." These are partially marching orders from Mr. Horowitz. During our appointment last week, he wouldn't stop nagging me until I filled him in on everything happening with Drew. Even though he didn't call his suggestion a "grand gesture," I know he would approve of what the girls and I discuss. "And with Valentine's Day around the corner, I can't think of a better time to do this."

I feel a big hand clamp down on my shoulder, and I look up at my brother, Hawk. No doubt he's here to pick up his wife, Roxy. I can't help but notice the way she looks at him, her eyes overflowing with love. What I wouldn't give to make that my new norm with Drew.

"Hey, bro, what's new?" Hawk asks, more than a little surprised to see me attending the Hollister romance book club and taking notes.

I stand up, shaking his hand before enveloping him in a bear hug. "You're just the man I need to talk to. I need you to help me plan the ultimate grand gesture."

Hawk's face scowls, confused, as if I'm playing a practical joke on him. "Grand gesture? What's that?"

"Don't act so clueless, husband." Roxy pipes up. "You're exceedingly good at those."

"I am?" he asks, looking bewildered.

I pull an extra chair up to the table. "Sit down. We need to have a brainstorming session."

Chapter Nineteen

DREW

I check my phone discreetly between people walking up to the table where I sit, signing autographs of my book. I haven't had a text from Fletcher since first thing this morning when he sent his customary top-of-the-day message. Normally, that would be okay. After all, he's a very busy cardiologist.

But it's Valentine's Day...our first as a couple, and I hope he won't forget. It would feel too much like past relationships, even though everything about this past month has convinced me that Fletcher is different.

My heart sinks in my chest a little, wondering if he's okay. Another part of me recognizes a damning pattern in all of this. The beginning of a slow decline away from each other. Every day, one message less or one message shorter...

I hate to be fatalistic when it comes to relationships. It's a terrible look for a romance writer. But it's all I've ever known in real life.

A middle-aged woman with long brown hair approaches me, a huge stack of books in hand. When I first started writing IR romance, I assumed that my main audience would be black women. But I've been pleasantly surprised over the years to find that women of all colors and backgrounds enjoy what I write. I guess it shouldn't surprise me. Love is love, after all.

"Hi, I'm Drew," I say with a big smile, reaching out to shake her free hand.

She squeals instead of greeting me. "I am one of your biggest fans. Oh, my God! To see you in person is amazing. Beyond amazing. I could pinch myself!"

"Tell me your name," I say, grabbing the stack of books from her to begin signing as we talk.

"Jacinda."

"And, Jacinda, am I using your name when I sign these books?"

"Yes, please."

I make her spell it out just to be sure. Then, I start dedicating and signing each book as she tells me about her favorite characters and scenarios. "Your books always have the most romantic endings. I mean, that time Roland showed up at the high-rise building to whisk Tanika off her feet. And then he had to climb one hundred flights of stairs because the elevators were out of service. Oh my God! That was the best ending ever."

I laugh. "I'm so glad you enjoyed it. As I always say, why finish small when you can finish big?"

I close the cover of another signed book, stacking it on top of the previous one. I grab the next one in her pile, opening it to the title page, when the manager of the bookstore comes over with a strange look on her face.

She has a short black pixie cut and countless piercings in both ears and her nose and lips. "Is everything okay?" I ask, eyeing her with concern.

She nods before looking at the line of people ruefully and announcing, "Ms. Devereaux needs to step outside for a few minutes. So, we ask for your patience. If you'd like to follow her, that's fine. Or feel free to stay in line. Should you leave, however, please be sure to take a look at the person in front of and behind you so that you can easily find your place again afterward."

"Why do I need to go outside?" I ask, glancing between the manager and the line of fans snaking around the interior of the large, two-story bookstore in the heart of downtown San Diego.

"Because you're needed there."

My eyes shoot across the large lower floor of the bookstore past the shelves where Cassidy, my assistant, stands, shaking her head and shrugging. But there's a huge smile on her face that makes me suddenly suspicious.

Following the manager outside, we walk into the center of the parking lot as I register the sound of a helicopter's whirring blades overhead. No doubt the traffic bird out providing updates on an accident or delays. But then the manager looks up, shielding her eyes with her hand, and so do other readers in the crowd.

Realizing the helicopter is circling the parking lot, I do the same. To my surprise, a banner flows unfurled behind it. The words written on it catch my breath in my throat: "O'Day or Knight? Drew, Marry Me."

My hand comes reflexively to my mouth, and I stare long and hard at the banner, feeling my heart bounce in my chest. Some of my readers squeal, and others talk with animated hands, pointing at the romantic gesture. Suddenly, I feel a big, strong presence standing next to me.

Looking over, I see my handsome white cowboy in his black Stetson with his best Wranglers, button-down shirt, tooled boots, and shiny rodeo belt buckle. He holds a dozen purple roses in one hand and a small black velvet box in the other. As my eyes meet his, my hand still covering my mouth, he smiles from ear to ear.

God, I've missed this man's face. Even though he was here a week ago. Getting down on one knee, the big, burly physician looks me straight in the face, saying, "Well, sexy, what'll it be? O'Day or Knight? Either way, will you do me the honor of marrying me and spending the rest of your life as my bride?"

I drop down onto both knees in front of him before he can stop me. Tears flow down my cheeks as I nod enthusiastically, wrapping my arms around him and capturing his kissable, gorgeous lips with mine. "Yes," I whisper breathlessly. "Yes, baby, I'll marry you. And I'll spend the rest of my life with you, and I'll become Drew Knight."

He returns my kiss, holding me so close that I can feel his heart beating. "I love you more than life itself," he whispers.

"I love you, too, Fletcher. Forever."

He stands up, handing the roses to Cassidy, who stands nearby. Then, he offers me his hand, hoisting me into the air and twirling me around. The readers who followed us outside cheer along with the manager of the bookstore and a handful of other employees.

Leaning into me, he whispers against the shell of my ear, "I knew there was something missing when it came to our relationship. A beat or two we skipped. I wasn't down with the third-act breakup, though. No fucking way because it would break me in ways I don't even want to think about. But the grand gesture? I could get behind that. What do you think, Drew? Did I do okay?"

"You did better than okay, Fletcher. You did perfectly. Never has another living person made me feel so loved and cherished. Keep stuff like this up, and I'm going to have to include you as a co-writer on future books."

He laughs deep in his chest, and I savor feeling the rumble run through me. "We've got another grand gesture on its way at our wedding, you know."

I arch my eyebrow. "Wait, you just proposed, and you're already planning our wedding?"

"Just the entertainment. Mr. Horowitz is doing everything he can to change his lifestyle and strengthen his body and heart because he's hellbent on playing at our wedding."

"Seriously?" I ask, savoring the warmth and love the thought of this brings. "A matchmaker and musician. I can't think of a better man to have when we tie the knot."

"Good because I want and need you so badly, sexy. I don't want to wait any longer for you. So, let's get this wedding show on the road because I'm ready for you to help me write the best happily ever after the world has ever seen, whether it's in Hollister, LA, or somewhere else."

"I'm an expert at writing happily ever afters," I say with a huge smile.

He kisses me with relish, sheltering me in his arms and making me feel like the most loved and cherished heroine to ever grace the pages of a romance. And he reminds me through his tender kisses and warm whispers of affection that sometimes the best endings are one hundred percent authentically real and wonderfully unexpected.

* * *

Can't get enough of Drew and Fletcher? Read an exclusive bonus scene at this link: https://www.engrideaves.com/free bies/

* * *

Intrigued by the rumors circulating about Effie and Rock, the town good girl and bad boy? Discover the next sizzling install-ment in the Rough & Ready Country series, *Love at First Doubt*: https://www.engrideaves.com/love-at-first-doubt/

Or explore the Rough & Ready Country series, available now in KU: https://www.engrideaves.com/rough-ready-country/

Want to know more about Shelby and Farzad's romance? Dive into *Gifted to the Mountain Man*, a multicultural, steamy Christmas romance available now on KU: https://a.co/d/guhomII.

And for more spicy Christmas stories, check out *Mountain Man Santa* another scintillating read from the Rough & Ready Country world. Available now in KU: https://a.co/d/8cKENGT.

Also by Engrid Eaves

ROUGH & READY COUNTRY

Love at First Blizzard - He's a reclusive mountain man who runs a husky rescue, but his world gets turned upside down by the curvy classical musician he saves from a freak March blizzard.

Love at First Campfire - She's a headstrong, curvy true crime reporter who's never needed anybody until a handsome search and rescue unit lead risks everything to save her.

Love at First Rescue - He's a small-town sheriff who plays by the rules until his sexy dispatcher changes up the game, initiating a rescue that sets long-time passions ablaze.

Love at Second Chance - She's the new home health nurse in Rough & Ready Country, but miles of history with the grumpy ranch foreman are in danger of reigniting, despite her best intentions.

Love at First Baby - He's a wildland firefighter who refuses to settle down for anyone until the curvy hometown sweetheart and an unexpected baby make him reconsider what and who he's living for.

Love and Forgiveness - She's a museum director trying to move on until her estranged husband's security company wins her facility's contract, resurrecting long-buried passions.

Love at First Relationship - Everything about Flynn's paralegal, Jasmine, is off-limits as his much younger, inexperienced employee. But a fake relationship proposal quickly blossoms into much more.

Love at First House - A marriage of convenience is the only way to help Turner's neighbor keep her family together. He tells himself it's a practical arrangement, but his heart has other plans.

Love at First Night - He's a helicopter pilot crushing on his best friend's little sister, Roxy. A cataclysmic night gives them a glimmer into a world of possibilities, but will love or heartbreak prevail?

Love at First Beat - Army cardiologist, Fletcher, excels at healing... But matters of the heart are another thing. Until he meets Drew, a romance writer, who specializes in happy endings.

Love at First Doubt - Kindergarten teacher, Effie, knows the town bad boy, Rock, is trouble. A tattoo artist and rockabilly musician, the cowboy's all wrong for the wholesome curvy girl. Or is he?

Love at First Wedding

Love at First Secret

Love at First Revenge

Love and Redemption

ROUGH & READY LAWMEN

Possessed by the Bounty Hunter - A six-figure bounty draws me back to my ex-fiancée and her mafia-linked Creole family. Soon, a centuries-old curse blurs the line between hunter and hunted.

LOG CABIN CHRISTMAS

Gifted to the Mountain Man - Farzad's first Christmas stateside is lonely until the woman he can't stop thinking about needs protection. As sparks fly, will his cabin and heart be big enough for two?

NAUGHTY & SPICE

Mountain Man Santa - A blizzard leaves Jerry snowed in with his curvy server, Stacey. She may not be ready for commitment...or the secrets of his dark past. But naughty or nice, he won't stop until she's all his...

About the Author

Engrid Eaves publishes short, sweet, and steamy romances featuring gruff alpha male protectors and the headstrong, curvy girls they fall head over heels for.

Her heroes may have painful pasts, but they always find forever with their soulmates. Sexy, satisfying, heartfelt happily ever afters guaranteed!

If you'd like to stay in touch or get your next delicious mountain man, curvy girl romance fix (and who doesn't?), sign up for her newsletter: www.engrideaves.com.

goodreads.com/engrideaves

bookbub.com/profile/engrid-eaves

instagram.com/engrid_eaves

tiktok.com/@authorengrideaves

facebook.com/EngridEavesAuthor